I0679787

A House

But Not a Home

By Edward J Funk

Contents

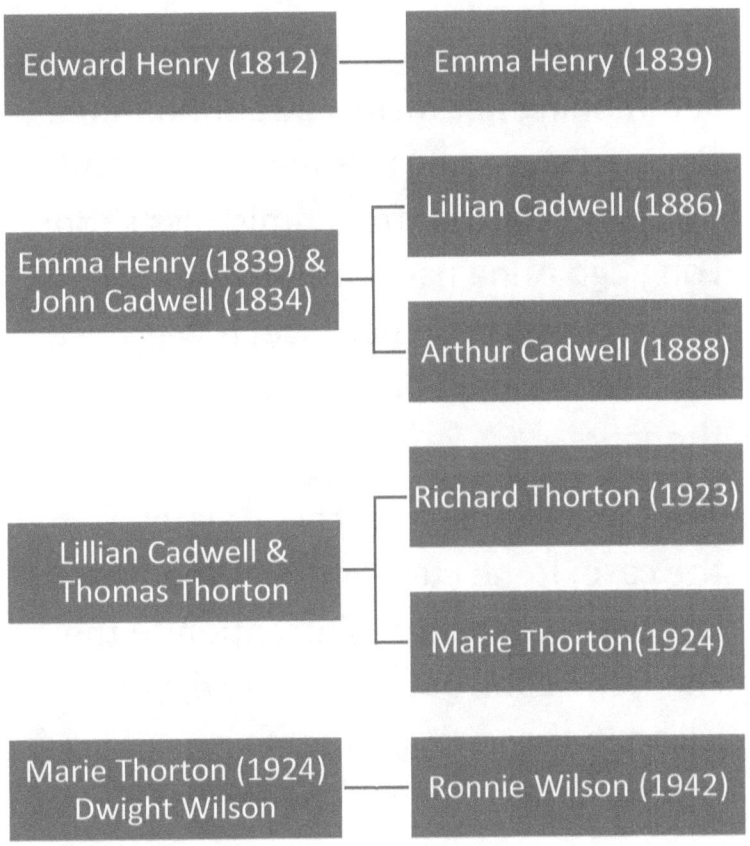

Edward Henry (1812) — Emma Henry (1839)

Emma Henry (1839) & John Cadwell (1834)
- Lillian Cadwell (1886)
- Arthur Cadwell (1888)

Lillian Cadwell & Thomas Thorton
- Richard Thorton (1923)
- Marie Thorton(1924)

Marie Thorton (1924) Dwight Wilson — Ronnie Wilson (1942)

Chapter One: The Jewell House

Irene rang her bell in an agitated manner, summoning her maid's attention. Anna stopped sweeping the stair carpet and dutifully reported to her mistress's room. Long ago Anna had learned not to show any expression on her face; it was best that Irene would not be able to read her thoughts.

"Yes, Miss Irene, how can…"as so often the case, Irene cut her off. "When's the last time you paid any attention to the children? Look out the window, you'll see Lillian in the yard, and some riffraff boy's staring at her through the fence."

"Yes, Miss Irene. I'll go out right away and coax Lillian onto the porch." Anna knew better than to explain that she had no notion that Lucille, the tutor, had finished with Lillian's lessons for the afternoon. Best to deal with the mistress in the most simplistic way possible.

This interchange took place on a pleasant spring day in the town of Richland, Indiana, 1893. The setting was the largest house in town. To explain why this was so, one needs to go back to Irene's grandfather.

Edward Henry arrived in northwestern Indiana in the mid-1850s, less than a decade after the Potawatomi Indians were forced to relocate to a reservation in Kansas. He arrived from Vermont with pockets bulging with cash. In a short period, he acquired 32,000 acres from government-affiliated land agents, and thus, commanded the largest cattle ranch east of the Mississippi.

Irene wasn't a commanding person, but she knew she was rich and that was enough for her. She left all financial considerations to her husband, Cyrus Jewell. He didn't come from significant wealth, but he loved money. He loved having it; he loved making it; he even liked to see his wife spend it, as long as she got permission from him first.

Their house mirrored their wealth and the esteem of their social standing. A Queen Anne design, it was a wooden structure of three stories with a pitched blue-shingled roof, situated on a commanding half of a square block lot. It had a ballroom on the third floor, a music room just off the entrance foyer, a huge living room, an enormous dining room, a kitchen designed for sumptuous entertaining, five bedrooms, plus servants' quarters. The exterior exhibited a roomy wrap-around porch in proper scale with the house, a roofed area on the east side where one could alight into a carriage, no matter the weather, and a fence of aligned silver iron spears that enclosed the whole property. There was a carriage house and stable behind the house, and next to that a large kitchen garden. Adjacent to the garden, the huge lot also afforded space for an orchard of fruit trees. Shrubs and seasonal flowers waved along the contour of the front porch.

In addition to Anna, the maid, and Lucille, the tutor, there was a cook named Margaret, a downstairs maid named Alice, who also helped in the kitchen, and a stableman named John.

Cyrus was quite pleased to finance such a house as he saw it as a temple to himself. After all, people were already calling it the Jewell House. And why not? Irene, maiden name Cadwell, may have inherited wealth, but he had made it grow and grow. Everything he touched was golden, from Chicago bank stocks, to Chinese railroad bonds.

Most of their agrarian neighbors were immigrants living hardscrabble lives, so Irene was somewhat limited in finding people of their social status to entertain. Basically she was limited to her own relations, and the families into which they had married.

Theirs was a loveless marriage that, nevertheless, gave each of them what they wanted. Irene had grown up indulged, and as long as that continued, all was well. As for Cyrus, the absence of love only made his fiduciary focus sharper.

Not surprisingly, they were indifferent parents to their two children. Lillian had been born in 1886 and her brother, Arthur, in 1888. Both children resembled their father, who had intense, dark, good looks; features that looked much better on Arthur.

On that spring afternoon when Irene had sent Anna to summon Lillian from the yard, Arthur was already playing on the porch, something Irene had not been able to see from her second-story window. Besides, it wasn't so much that she was concerned where her children were, as much as the possibility that Lillian might have been contaminated by the "common" boy on the other side of the fence.

Anna called out as soon as she passed through the double front doors, "Lillian, dear, your mother wants you to come up to the porch and play." Lillian looked at Anna and then up at the open window in her mother's room, and knew she best comply; otherwise Anna would be in trouble.

Lillian was to address Irene as mother, never Mom or Mama. At age seven, she already knew some basic things about her mother. One, that her mother's whims often made no sense, and two, even if the word indifferent wasn't part of Lillian's vocabulary, she knew very well what it meant. She also read her father's parental efforts in the same light, and adjusted her expectations accordingly.

This insight was unavailable to her five-year-old brother, Arthur, who was still looking to his parents for love. Lillian sensed this, and knew it made Arthur vulnerable. She felt very protective of him.

Both were now on the porch, and Arthur was underneath a white wicker table pretending it was his house. Lillian, getting into the spirit of things, said, "Artie, in school today, Miss Lucille was telling me about Florida, where it's summer all year long, and people have homes right next to the ocean. Kids go out every day and splash and swim, and their fathers catch fish for supper. Let's pretend the porch is the ocean and we can turn some of these chairs over and pretend that there are several houses on the shore. We'll walk out into the water and take a swim, and maybe we can catch some fish by our hands. Oranges grow in Florida, so we'll pick a few of those to have with dinner. I'll go fishing and maybe you could build a fire on the shore so that we could cook them."

Arthur, quick to join in the fantasy, stated, "Maybe I should pick the oranges first."

"Good idea."

"But Lil, where is the orange tree?"

"There's one right next to your house. Don't you see it?"

"Oh, yes. Now I do!"

They both got busy, first with a swim, then Lillian catching the fish, followed by Arthur picking oranges, and then both of them cooking the fish.

They sat in Artie's wicker house, now a Florida house, and pretended to eat their meal. "This is the best fish I've ever tasted," cried Artie.

"I didn't know oranges could taste this sweet," exclaimed Lillian.

Then Arthur asked, "But there's no maid. Who's going to wash the dishes?"

"That's no problem. We'll just rinse them in the ocean," and they proceeded with the task.

At seven, Lillian seldom inhabited the world of imagination unless it was with Artie. She'd do anything for him.

The following year, Arthur began his tutelage under Miss Lucille. He was not nearly as precocious as Lillian, who was quick with math. One way Lucille was able to teach him to count to big numbers was to take him in the yard and help him count all the vertical iron rods of the fence that surrounded the property. It easily took him to over five hundred. Arthur did become a competent reader once he understood that books could take him places that stretched his imagination.

There was a grand piano in the music room, and Arthur asked Lucille to teach him to play. He quickly learned what she was capable of teaching, and with remarkable rapidity and skill, continued to teach himself.

Early on, Irene had instructed Lucille to teach the children French, stating that it had been part of her education, and that she was very proud of her facility in the language. Lucille then thought that Irene might appreciate her addressing her using very simple French phrases, but quickly realized that Irene had no idea of what she was talking about. As the maid, Anna, had learned, the simplest form of communication with Irene was the most effective.

Cyrus had little communication with the children, or really, anyone in the household other than to bark orders at the servants. If he did notice the children, it was in the most cursory fashion.

One day when Lillian was twelve and Arthur ten, both were sitting in the garden, working on assignments given them by Miss Lucille. Arthur put down his book and looking at Lillian, said, "Father doesn't like me."

The pain in his voice cut through Lillian. With her penchant for clarity, she knew that Arthur's observation was true. But counter to her usual proclivity for honesty, she said "Artie, Father only thinks about business; he's not thinking much about either of us."

Whereas Lillian had high intelligence; Arthur had a poetic sensitivity. He replied, "But when he does take notice, he looks at us differently. Toward you, he sees himself. Toward me, he sees a failure. I don't think there's anything I can do about it."

When she realized the degree of Artie's anguish, Lillian put down her book, then got up and kneeled before his chair. She took his hand in hers and responded with a force from somewhere deep within: "Listen Artie, we're in this together.

We're all we have in this world, but we'll always have each other." With a pleading look in her eyes, she asked, "Do you understand that?"

A sense of peace cascaded through Arthur's body. He had always felt safest in his big sister's presence, but now the idea that she would always be there took on almost mystical power. He quietly replied to her query, "Yes Lil, I think I do."

Arthur learned something else that afternoon: that their exchange was reciprocal. He didn't quite know how, but Lillian convinced him that he was giving her something just as important as what she had been giving him.

Both children felt that their parents were literally keeping them in a cage. The iron-rodded fence that surrounded the property enclosed them as if they were a zoo attraction. If fact, the town kids would often gather on the streetside and stare at them. Their unabashed stares suggested they thought Lillian and Arthur didn't have the capacity to know that they were on display.

What made this isolation so unnecessary was that there was a school in town they could have attended. Granted they would not have had the individual attention they received from Miss Lucille, but the socialization would have offered some trade-off. Also, they could have gone to Sunday school, but that too was unavailable to them. These decisions were driven by Irene's fear of contamination. Cyrus wasn't concerned enough to care.

One year followed another: Irene spending much of the time in her room being waited upon, Cyrus occupying a room originally planned as a dressing room attached to his bedroom that had been re-fashioned as an office. There were three separate phone lines into the house; one downstairs, one in Irene's dressing room, and one in Cyrus's office. By far, the one most used, and from Cyrus's point of view, the only one used for any matter of importance, was his own.

Two or three times a year, they entertained on a grand scale, even employing the ballroom on the third floor. An eight-piece orchestra was hired from Lafayette, as were white-jacketed waiters who served the hors d'oeuvres, dinner, and various liquors and wines.

Cyrus was supportive of this extravagance because, once again, he saw it as a reflection of himself. That, plus, some of the guests were men he did business with, or wanted to do business with. Irene was her most alive during these parties; she always knew this was the life she was meant to live.

Early in the evening, Lillian and Arthur, dressed in their best, were presented to the guests. They took no joy in this ritual. They correctly understood the phoniness of the situation; neither parents nor guests cared one hoot if they were there or not.

As life continued in the Jewell House, it was a dreary one considering the relationships between the parents and children. But Irene and Cyrus were so self-consumed; it was quite possible they didn't understand the very human, very loving relationship between their two children. Lillian protected Arthur's realm where he could continue to live in a creative world. To her betterment, some of his enchantment rubbed off on her, clearly a benefit to her serious nature.

Margaret, the cook, came down with the flu in the spring of 1902. Lillian and Cyrus found this very inconsiderate. They were now reduced to the maid, Alice's, efforts in the kitchen, which were decidedly unsatisfactory. They had sent Margaret out of the house to stay with her sister and her sister's family, until she was recovered.

A week later, while putting Arthur to bed, Anna realized he was burning up with a fever. His temperature was taken and registered at 104 degrees. The doctor was called immediately, and given the home where the call originated, he arrived within minutes. It's not that the doctor did not care about all his patients, he did. But he had responded to so many flu patients in the community, patients with whom he had tried every remedy he could think of, and was honest enough to know there was very little he could do. He collected some sputum to study later under his microscope to confirm the diagnosis (but he was already sure), and he gave Arthur acetylsalicylic acid to reduce the fever. Arthur hadn't complained of the pain, but the doctor knew he was experiencing it.

Neither Irene nor Cyrus entered the sick room, although Irene looked in from the door from time to time. Lillian was absolutely forbidden to go near Arthur's room. It was mostly Anna who sat with him, relieved from time to time by Alice.

Anna knew the bond between sixteen-year-old Lillian and fourteen-year-old Arthur, and after Lillian pleaded with her to permit a quick visit, she allowed them a few private moments. Lillian was shocked to see how wasted Arthur looked. She knew she'd only have a few minutes with him so she prepared what she wanted to say, but was now having a hard time saying anything. This was made all the more difficult by the look Arthur was giving her. It was both beautiful but at the same time so honest that it was intimidating. Lillian began, "Artie, do you remember the afternoon we were sitting in the garden and we pledged we'd always be there for each other? That you and I were all each of us had? That's why

I know you're going to pull through this. You promised me, and you've never broken a promise."

Arthur replied with a sweet smile. But it was the peaceful smile of one who had lived his life, and knew it was about to end. He said, "I will always be there for you; I can see that now." He then looked directly into her eyes and said, "Lil, I'm not afraid to die."

Lillian fought her tears, not wanting Arthur to see the depth of her sadness. She bent down and kissed him on the forehead and then left him in the tranquil state he had now entered. She never saw him alive again.

Chapter Two: Surprises

The funeral was an exhibition. Arthur's open casket was placed in the entrance foyer, and as their wealthy friends came to call, Irene, dressed in black, could not contain her demonstrations of grief. She might have even believed them sincere. Cyrus had always seen Arthur as weak. He now felt his death was a kind of embarrassment, certainly a poor reflection on the family.

Lillian, the sincere griever, tried to imagine a world without Arthur. She could not. She knew she had to get out of the house, and the following year, enrolled in the Evanston College for Women, located in Evanston, Illinois. It was a private school on the same grounds as Northwestern University. Her mother was indifferent to Lillian's higher education, but Cyrus always knew that it would be his daughter who carried his superior genes.

Lillian knew it too. That is, looking at both of her parents, she much more identified with her father's serious interests as opposed to her mother's frivolous pursuits. And with her natural aptitude for math, understanding financial matters came easily to her. She also had his drive, and, if not driven by the same hungers, she was still willing to work as hard.

Lillian took as many courses related to finance and investments as the curriculum offered. They opened her mind to ways to grow wealth that her father hadn't ever considered. They also opened her mind to a goal of financial independence from both her parents.

And, unlike her father, she began to realize that there were other things one could do with wealth beyond expanding it. However, that would have to wait until she became more independent.

Cyrus had hoped Lillian would meet a wealthy young man at Northwestern so that he'd have a son-in-law he'd be proud of. It didn't work out that way. She did meet wealthy young men, but she saw her father in them, ambitious to prosper from her financial advantages. Her mother had been willing to forfeit her landed-fortune to Cyrus in a trade-off that allowed her to remain a pampered child. Lillian would do no such thing. She was confident that she'd always have the ability to take care of herself.

Irene had never been a woman of surprise, but she came up with a doozy in the last week of Lillian's senior year. She died. She was only forty-three-years old, and the doctor said it was a heart attack brought on by stress. People found the explanation incredulous; what in her coddled life had ever been stressful?

Cyrus was in for another surprise. Irene had only owned the vast landholdings as a life estate. It would then pass along to her children in joint tenancy or, in the case of one surviving child, sole ownership. It seemed that Irene's mother knew her daughter's fickle nature, and was more confident that Irene's children, totally unknown to her, would manage the holdings with more sense. *Bark and Bark*, a firm of local lawyers, from the nearby town of Benton, had drawn the will. Cyrus had always shown disdain for the firm, and, in turn, they were just waiting for the years to pass for him to get his comeuppance.

Cyrus didn't mourn Irene at her funeral, but he did mourn his loss of control. And soon after Irene was laid to rest, Lillian made it clear that she felt competent to manage the estate on her own. She also asked *Bark and Bark* to convey the delicate message to Cyrus that her inheritance included the ground on which the Jewell House was built.

Cyrus was incensed that the daughter, who in his mind he had lavished so much love and attention, was turning him out. But he certainly had plenty of money of his own, as he had always made his investments in his name only. Besides, the fact the land Edward Henry had acquired in the 1850s for ranching purposes, and had morphed into very rich farmland, held little interest to him. Cyrus now looked at all things agrarian as primitive. His business genius was meant for more canny investments.

Unable to bear the thought that people would learn that Lillian was in charge, Cyrus moved to Chicago. He bought a brownstone on State Street, alerting those who might notice, that he was a wealthy man.

Lillian invited the tenant farmers in, one by one. It was a rare occurrence for any of the locals to get inside the Jewell House, but Lillian wanted to make them feel appreciated. She also wanted to evaluate them. Cyrus would have considered this kind of personal attention beneath his dignity.

Her business-inquisitive mind took her far beyond her farmlands, and far beyond the borders of the United States. Aware of the construction of the Panama Canal, she realized that extensive warehousing would need to be built in the major port cities of California. Over a six-week period, she traveled by train to visit Los Angeles and San Francisco to meet with agents whom she felt had a pulse on the best locations. But even more importantly, she wanted to find agents who could be trustworthy to deal with on a long-distance basis.

Now that Cyrus was out of her way, Lillian had a desire to make money to satisfy her own hungers. While she was a student at Evanston College for Women, she became aware of Hull House, a settlement house in Chicago that had been founded in 1889 by Jane Addams and Ellen Starr. Its purpose was to serve recently arrived European immigrants, and its reach was expanding rapidly, thanks to donors large and small. Lillian was one of the largest. She took great pride in doing something generous for others, something that would have never crossed Cyrus's mind. She was also happy to be part of something that had been started by two women, and that their efforts were changing the lives of so many.

Lillian was in no hurry to marry, if at all, and passed through her twenties feeling quite content on the subject. Her own parents' marriage had been a disaster, and she didn't feel she needed a man in the way many women did.

In her early thirties, when she did start thinking about it, one man kept surfacing in her mind. His name was Thomas Thorton. He was born in 1880 and was five years older than Lillian. He grew up in a wealthy home, and as had been the case with Irene, the money came through his mother's family landholdings. They also owned a grain elevator Thomas's maternal grandfather had built.

His father, not content with wealth generated from the land and the elevator, started dabbling in the future's market and became the first in their part of the country to lose almost everything. The elevator was all that was left, and now Thomas was in charge of its operations. He had a reputation for unflinching honesty.

Lillian had known Thomas all her life. When his family still had money, they were invited to join in the glitter of Irene's entertaining. Lillian had always liked him; he had a quiet dignity that made him stand out.

She invited him to dinner one evening under the guise that they could talk business, related to how Lillian was selling her grain. Lillian took notice of something she already knew; Thomas was quite good-looking. He was tall for the times, almost six feet, had blonde hair and blue eyes, the shade one often saw in spring skies.

Later that night, Lillian asked herself, "Could I really fall in love with Thomas?" She couldn't honestly say yes, but concluded that it would probably be the closest she would ever come. She knew herself well enough that she'd always have to be the lead horse in any relationship. And she knew Thomas well enough that he could accept that.

He reminded her of Arthur, the only person she had ever really loved. Both Arthur and Thomas existed on their own plane, one on which they were content, even if others were not capable of grasping. That had been so obvious with Arthur in his last hours, in the way he faced death with such peace.

She invited Thomas back the following week. After dinner they gathered in the music room, and sitting on the divan, Lillian was about to offer a proposition. Thomas surprised her by making one of his own. He professed, "Lillian, we've always known each other, and have always liked each other. We've both made choices that suggest we'll be spending the rest of our lives in this community. What would you say if we spent them together?"

With a big smile, uncharacteristic of Lillian, she responded. "Thomas, did you know I was about to suggest the same thing?"

"I felt last week that we were both thinking along the same lines. I've had a week more to think about it. I think we can make a very successful marriage out of being best friends. We can be very supportive of each other in ways only possible by the fact we've known each other our entire lives.

"I know that you are going to run your business affairs your way. That's fine with me. I'm confident you'll do a good job and besides, they're really none of my business. I'll run my business my way, and I know you'll respect that. After hesitating for a moment, he said, "Besides, I've always found you attractive!"

Lillian least expected this last proclamation, but knowing Thomas as she did, she knew his sentiment was totally honest. Feeling desired in this way made her feel different than she had ever felt before. She looked Thomas straight in the eyes and replied in a soft tone, "The answer is yes!" Thomas pulled her into an embrace and kissed her with surprising intensity that belied his calm demeanor.

They married in a small ceremony held in Lillian's garden. The year was 1920. Lillian was thirty-four and Thomas thirty-nine. They had hoped for a baby right away, but just as soon as they were giving up hope, their firstborn was on its way. He was born in 1923 and they named him Richard. No question about it, he looked very much like his dad. Lillian was relieved. She still carried childhood scars, and it would have been challenging if she gave birth to a child that looked like either of her parents.

Unfortunately, that is what happened a year later when her daughter was born. As the child grew, she had such a strong resemblance to Irene that Lillian often had to take a deep breath every time she saw her. She knew this attitude was very unfair. She named the little girl Marie after the famous physicist/chemist Madame Curie, and hoped that the girl's aspirations might eventually follow the same kind of intellectual curiosity.

When the children reached school age, they were not to be segregated in a cage like she and Arthur had been. She enrolled them in the local public school. She knew that they'd realize they were the rich family in town, but she also hoped they'd get to know other kids well enough to form relationships. And within reason, they were free to visit the local merchants whose stores were less than two blocks away.

Richard and Marie's path to adulthood led them along routes that were, to some degree, pre-determined. Richard was good looking, a good student, and manifested a work ethic from a very young age. Marie, who did look more and more like her grandmother Irene, struggled as a student, and consequently, shied away from academic challenges.

Unlike her grandmother, and underneath her insecurities, Marie had a good nature. More than anything, she longed for a sense of belonging.

It was much easier for Lillian to bond with Richard. He was everything she wanted a son to be, which included being as strong-willed as she. And he had a disarming smile that could melt her heart, even against her will. It scared her a bit, but it also made her feel alive and hopeful.

Early on, she realized Marie would be no Madame Curie and accepted that. But the two of them had a difficult time connecting. Marie most wanted tenderness from her mother; something Lillian was incapable of giving. And Lillian intimidated Marie; it was as simple as that.

In his quiet way, Thomas was a good father to both his children. He was proud of Richard's many accomplishments and was willing to affirm them. He was also willing to direct his son onto a track of humility when his ego was getting the best of him.

Thomas had a very different parenting task with Marie. First and foremost, she needed to know she was loved. She got that from him. But it wasn't quite enough, because Marie knew what everyone in town knew, that her mother was the apex of the family strength. For someone as fragile as Marie, this reality undermined her foundations.

Thomas and Lillian had a much better marriage than was generally understood. From the outside, it looked like they both continued living the same lives they had before they married. But as Thomas had predicted, a marriage based on friendship could be very successful. And people would have been surprised to learn that their lovemaking was more than satisfactory.

Thomas continued running the grain elevator with integrity, and Lillian continued to prosper in her business interests. Besides the farmland, which people knew about, her fortune grew in ways they did not. She expanded the profitable California warehouses and discarded those less successful. And in the early 30s, Lillian started gobbling up radio stations. By the end of the decade, she owned WOWO in Fort Wayne, WIAS in Cincinnati, and WLW in Columbus, Ohio.

Also, in the late thirties, both her children had started high school. Lillian had big plans for Richard; as for Marie, she just hoped that she would be able to make it through her senior year.

Chapter Three: Richard and Helen

Richard was quite popular with the girls; he really didn't have to try. His athletic good looks combined with his easy charm were obvious. And, of course, there was the money. All through his school years, whether people were willing to admit it or not, he was viewed through the prism of money.

Dating for most high-schoolers in Richland often involved getting together with friends, listening to music on the radio, and when a car was available, going to Benton or Newton for movies. While watching the movie, a guy might "accidentally" touch his date in a stimulating fashion, hoping more would come later.

Richard started dating at sixteen and had quite an advantage over other guys in that he owned his own car. The 1938 yellow Ford Coupe wasn't the most expensive car on the road, but nevertheless, it drew a lot of attention as it was the only one in town. Any girl he asked out felt privileged, and her parents were hopeful that a merger with the wealthiest family in town was in the offing. If the hour was getting just a little late, they may have been encouraged that the young couple was out parking somewhere, their passions getting the better of them.

But that wasn't happening. Richard enjoyed the company of the girls he dated, and his hormones were pumping at similar rates of other adolescent males, but he was very measured in how he acted upon them.

Probably none of his dates were all that surprised; Richard was very measured in all his interactions with schoolmates, female and male. He enjoyed easy banter with them, laughed at their jokes, and was spiritedly engaged in sports. Sports, for the small town of Richland, meant basketball. With his height, he was a natural as the center on the team. But after playing hard on the floor, the deliberate Richard soon reappeared in the locker room.

The grade school and the high school were combined in one building, and in the 1930s, the enrollment for the whole school never reached 100. Of this enrollment, the majority were country kids transported by school buses.

Everyone in the school knew everyone else. The seniors in high school may not have bothered to learn the names of the first-graders, but they knew who they were. They would have known who their older siblings were and who their parents were. In time the kids would know what families were related, and many of them were. The whole community was like a family that had been interwoven for generations. And if you were town kids, after school and during the summers, you were in and out of each other's homes as if they were your own.

That wasn't true for Richard and Marie. They didn't play in other children's homes, and most definitely, other children did not play in theirs. And yes, their family had been there longer than anyone's; Richard's great-great-grandfather Edward Henry had at one time owned most of the land of the surrounding area. But they had never joined in relationships between neighbors, like farmers helping each other with threshing wheat or shocking oats. The families of the Jewell House never married their neighbors, and they never spent Sunday afternoons with neighbors, playing croquet in the yard and gossiping on the porch.

Instead, they were the favorite subject of gossip. Was the relationship between Lillian and Thomas really a marriage? Was Richard as full of himself as many assumed? What was going on with Marie? She seemed a bit off, or was she just slow? And most of all, what was Lillian doing with all that money?

The focus on Lillian's money had intensified through the 30s as the country was reeling from the shock of the Depression. The price of corn dropped to a dime a bushel, hogs that farmers raised couldn't bring the cost of freight to ship them to market, and the mortgage man was breathing hard down their necks. The town merchants were barely better off, as their customers couldn't pay their bills.

The tenant farmers on Lillian's farms were treated more than fairly. None were displaced, and she quietly subsidized them to keep them afloat. Thomas acted as the agent for these transactions, and made it very clear that they were not to discuss the matter with anyone. In a small community, to require this kind of secrecy was a tall order, but the weights of Lillian's mystery and wealth were powerful enough for the secrecy to succeed.

So, even though Lillian owned all her farms outright, they still presented losses during the Depression. Her income from the warehouses also diminished, but sales of air time on her radio stations zoomed. Her charitable giving also increased dramatically, and she increased her support for the Hull House, which by now, had spurred dozens of other settlement houses. She also had faith in the Red Cross and gave generously.

Young Lillian and her brother Arthur had felt like animals in a zoo when the town children would stare at them through the iron-barred fence. Lillian and Thomas meant to correct that by sending their children to the local school. But the family wealth metaphorically formed another cage. They were still being stared at, if not visibly, certainly as invasively.

Consequently, it really wasn't hard to understand why Richard was so measured in his interactions with his peers...they really weren't his peers. With his deliberate manner, he seemed to find a balance by which he could manage his life.

Marie was less fortunate. She really didn't fit in anywhere. Not at home because her parents and her brother were so much brighter. And not at school, because she came from a different world. She struggled with everything and felt very insecure. And because she was so insecure, she felt it was her fault.

Shortly after Richard began his senior year, he began to take notice of a girl named Helen. She had chestnut-brown hair, blue eyes and a quiet demeanor. When she did speak, it was in a gentle voice. Richard had always known who she was; she was the daughter of one of Lillian's tenant farmers, but he now realized that all through their school years together, he didn't know her. He wondered if anyone did, and that intrigued him.

One Thursday as they were leaving the school cafeteria simultaneously, he said, "Helen, wait a moment. There's something I'd like to ask you." Whereas other girls usually responded to any attention he would give them with an inviting gaze, Helen's response was to look at him openly. A little surprised, but at the same time liking her reaction, he asked, "What I wanted to know is if you'd like to go to a movie with me this Saturday. We could go to Benton or we could go to Newton. I've checked; the one playing in Newton is called 'The Strange Case of Dr. Kildare.' The one in Benton has Spencer Tracy playing Thomas Edison. Would you like to see either of those?"

"It's very kind of you to ask me, Richard, but I've already committed to baby-sit this Saturday. It's for the Harry Datzmans. They've been very generous in using me as a sitter, and I wouldn't want to let them down." Helen started walking away, but then she turned back for a second, and with a slight smile, said, "I hope you ask me for another time, but it might work better if you ask me earlier in the week."

Richard smiled back; he admired Helen for how she had just handled the situation. Then he wondered if she had been on many dates, but decided that really didn't make any difference. He wanted to go out with her. Next time, he would ask earlier in the week.

On the first date, Richard found himself very much wanting to kiss her, but did not attempt anything in the car as he feared she'd find that off-putting. Instead, his first attempt was just as he walked her to the door. She was receptive, but she didn't kiss him back. This was repeated on their next couple of dates.

There were dances held in the gymnasium periodically, and Richard asked her to attend one for the following Saturday. When they arrived, other students were startled to see them together. There had been rumors that they had gone out a few times, but there was an assumption that Richard wouldn't want to be seen with her in such a public way. Some speculated that Helen had been willing to go "all the way," but that still wouldn't explain why he'd bring her to a dance.

Besides, Helen had always seemed so reserved. By the time of their senior year, Richard's classmates assumed that it would take a much more aggressive temptress to finally get Richard to cut loose sexually.

However, Richard and Helen did have normal hormones and their relationship evolved to sexual play far beyond the point that Richard had ever engaged in before. The kissing and petting would eventually evoke passionately heavy breathing, but then Helen would bring it to a stop. After the fact, Richard was always grateful that she did because he had such respect for her. And unlike many dating couples their age, they spent a great deal of time pouring their hearts out to each other, expressing their hopes, their fears, and their innermost thoughts.

They started seeing each other not just on weekends but also on occasional week-nights. Lillian had generally left him to lead his own life, but with his increased absences, she wanted to know where he was, and more importantly, who he was with. So one night when he was coming in, she had waited up.

She came to the point. "Richard, where have you been?"

Richard told her, "Mom, I'm seeing the most wonderful girl. Her name is Helen Bennett."

Lillian immediately wanted to know, "Is her father Leonard Bennett?"

"Yes."

In a raised voice, Lillian said, "For God's sake Richard. You're dating the hired help!"

"Mom, you don't know her. I feel more comfortable with her than anyone in this community."

Lillian gave him a cynical look, and using more base language than he was used to hearing from her, said, "I hope you're not getting that comfortable. It would be the dream of any girl in your school to get pregnant with you as the father. Are you thinking with your head or your penis?"

Richard replied, "Mom, I'm surprised at you. I've always known that you live a parallel life to everyone in Richland, but I didn't think you were so judgmental. That you're such a snob!"

"Richard. Within reason, I've always made a point to not tell you what to do. I've wanted you to become your own man in the same way I've had to become my own woman. But for God's sake...a farm girl!"

Richard shot a look of disgust at his mom, but it didn't deter her from continuing, "You have to focus on your future. You'll be going to Northwestern and majoring in Business. And during those college years, you'll find a much larger world that will pull you toward your rightful place in it. You'll meet young women who will stimulate you in ways you can't even imagine now."

 "Mom, can't you be even a little bit reasonable?"

 "I'm not going to argue with you. You know how I feel about the matter." With that Lillian turned and walked away. She was grateful that Richard couldn't see the look of alarm on her face.

That night as Richard lay in bed, he picked up the play "Our Town," an assignment given by his English teacher, Mrs. McGuire. The story focused on a young couple living in a small New Hampshire town. The play, written by Thornton Wilder, had been a runaway hit in New York. Two passages spoken by George to

Emily, the two young high school lovers, caught his attention.

First passage:

> "I think that once you've found a person that you're very fond of . . . I mean a person who's fond of you, too, and likes you enough to be interested in your character. . . . Well, I think that's just as important as college is, and even more so."

And the second passage:

> "And, like you say, being gone all the time...in other places and meeting other people...Gosh, if anything like that can happen I don't want to go away. I guess new people aren't any better than old ones. I'll bet they almost never are, Emily...I feel that you're as good a friend as I've got. I

don't need to go and meet the people in other towns."

Richard had an eerie feeling reading those passages and felt that they came into his life on that particular night for a reason. And he pondered...

Thomas enjoyed working in the garden, and that's where Richard found him a few evenings later. They had a good father/son relationship, but like many fathers and sons, they didn't talk about a lot of personal matters. Richard finally got up the nerve to say, "Dad, I need to talk something over with you. I've been seeing this girl Helen Bennett, and I like her a lot. She's really quite special. Mom knows about it. She hasn't even met her, and yet she is very disapproving. That seems so unfair. I don't want to hurt

Mom, but I'm going to continue seeing Helen. My question to you is, how do I handle Mom?"

Thomas, who had been standing while listening to Richard, said, "Son, let's sit down in these chairs for a few minutes." Then he proceeded to reply, "There are two sides to this issue. Regarding your mom, be patient, give her time, and try to see if there is merit from her point of view." Richard, not liking what he was hearing, nevertheless, continued listening patiently.

"The second side of this discussion is about you. Obviously, you feel very strongly about Helen; you're at a stage in life where one does feel strongly. But, believe it or not, you're going to change so much in the next five to ten years. What I'm saying is to continue with the way you feel about Helen, but open your mind that you need more time to make mature decisions."

Richard really didn't appreciate this advice about himself either. He nodded his head to suggest that he had been listening, but as he walked away, he wondered very much if either of his parents had ever known what it was like to feel passionately in love. He very much doubted it.

What no one realized on that quiet, spring evening, in the town of Richland, was how crazy their little world was about to become.

Chapter Four: A Tiny Speck

Much of the world was already crazy. Japan had begun invading China in 1931 and now controlled much of that country. Germany had started their push to take over Europe by invading Czechoslovakia and Poland in 1939. Then in the spring of 1940, they overran Belgium, the Netherlands, Luxembourg and France. That would leave only Great Britain to fight back on the European front.

The people of the United States had little appetite for war. Just twenty years earlier, they had lost over 100,000 men in World War 1. In addition, they were still recovering from the Depression.

Richard continued to see Helen, and he didn't attempt any deceptions to keep his parents from knowing. Thomas hoped that his son would not make any rash decisions, and Lillian hoped that the summer would pass quickly. At least Richard didn't rebel about enrolling at Northwestern, and departed for Evanston in September, 1941.

On December 7th of that year, Japan bombed Pearl Harbor. The following day, the United States declared war on Japan. Three days later, Germany declared war on the United States and, only hours later, the United States declared war on Germany.

A year earlier, the United States had instituted the Selective Training and Service, an act which required men between the ages of 21 to 27 to register for the draft. Once the country had engaged in the war, a decision was made allowing men in college deferment long enough to finish the school year. There was already a movement to lower the draft age to eighteen, so the fact Richard could finish out the year provided little comfort to Lillian.

She decided to take action that few other mothers could. She discovered that certain jobs in agriculture exempted men whose work was considered essential. So even though Richard was still in Evanston, she named him executive in charge of her sizable agricultural interests. The claim held little legitimacy, but unspoken was her power over all the people employed by her farms. More than one served on the local draft board. Would they defy her?

The answer was no. When Richard came home for his semester break, and found out how his mom had manipulated his draft status, he became irate. He challenged her, "Apparently it's okay for other kids in this town to go to war and get blown to bits, but I'm too precious. I'm to be spared. How do you think you make me feel as a man? My mama's running interference between me and artillery fire."

Lillian responded, "I've only done what any mother would do."

Richard quickly retorted, "You're making my point. Because what you really just said was, "I've only done what any other mother would do...if they could!!!!!" But they can't! Can they? They don't have your money and your power. Do you have any idea how your money and power have screwed up my life from the day I was born?"

"Richard, I suggest you take a long walk until you've settled down. Apparently, you have a lot to think through."

"And you don't! There's to be no questioning of your actions!"

"I won't tolerate your talking to me this way."

"Oh, so here we go. I'm being dismissed. How many times have we been at this juncture? I question you, or say something you don't like, and I'm dismissed. I'm to go to my room or take a walk. I'm sure it doesn't matter, as long as I disappear. Well, I'm not going to disappear. For once in your life, you have to realize that your opinion isn't the only one that matters."

As had happened in other heated exchanges, when Richard refused to disappear, Lillian did. She left the living room and went upstairs to the safety of her bedroom suite.

Richard got into his car and drove to a secluded place where he and Helen often parked. It wasn't Avery Hill or Big Tree, two well-known destinations for lovers. They had found their own place and that made it all the more special to them.

He got out of the car and started walking. His mom had been right about one thing; he had a lot to think through.

As Richard walked, his thoughts regarding his mother's actions to keep him out of the draft flowed in circles. Had she acted because members of their family really didn't need to play by the same rules as everyone else? Or did she act out of love for him? Or could those two intentions be separated?

After walking for hours, he concluded that his feelings were so over-wrought, he'd need time to work through them. And that reflection was in competition with other questions pushing their way into his consciousness. Would he return to Northwestern to finish out the year? Would he follow an impulse to enlist immediately? And if he did, into which branch would he enlist?

After finishing his walk, he went to the Richland Library. It was one of the Andrew Carnegie-endowed libraries, a bequest very much appreciated by the citizens of the little town. First he read through national periodicals such as "Time" and "Life Magazine." He had already been vaguely aware of the speed in which Germany was absorbing its neighbors. He found it particularly alarming to read how quickly France had been overrun.

He then turned his attention to the war in the Pacific. Like many Americans, he had found it shocking when Japan had bombed Pearl Harbor two and a half months earlier. Why would they do that? Why would they purposely invite the United States into the war? What he was able to discern was that Great Britain's Navy had been forced to abandon their interests in Asia in order to protect the seas surrounding their home island. The United States Navy stepped in to patrol the waters around Malaya and the Dutch East Indies. Both of these locales could provide Japan with natural resources badly needed to continue their conquest of Asia.

Helen was a working girl by this time. After graduating the previous spring, she got a job working at the bus station in Newton. It was called the Post House and included a restaurant. Helen started out in the kitchen, but within weeks was elevated to a position of waitress/cashier.

Her parents had never gotten along...her dad's drinking didn't help... and Helen had been subjected to a lifetime of tension. So even though her hourly earnings were meager, she chose to spend a sizable portion renting a room in Newton. It provided a very small kitchen, but she was allowed to eat modest portions at the Post House. Her goal was to save enough money to eventually go to nursing school at Saint Elizabeth's in Lafayette.

On the day that Richard was walking and thinking, Helen was working a long shift and wouldn't get off until 10:00 p.m. They had made plans to meet after that.

When Richard met with Helen later that night, his disquieting thoughts of the afternoon immediately melted away. Just being with her took him to a place of equanimity. He knew that would happen. The whole world had recalibrated after the United States entered the war. What didn't change was Helen and Richard's love for each other. Neither could imagine that it wouldn't always exist between them.

Once they had parked, they got into the back seat. Richard very much wanted to take their lovemaking to completion. Helen seemed to understand, but when the momentum reached the point of seemingly no return, she said, "Please, Richard, no." Those were not words he wanted to hear, and he continued to massage her thighs. Helen removed his hand, kissed it, but made it clear that she wanted him to stop. It took Richard a few moments, but in the end, he reluctantly respected her wishes.

On another day, when Helen had the afternoon off, they took a long walk in the country. Richard had spent more time in the library and after reading all he could, decided that he wanted to enlist. He was leaning toward the Marines, as the war in the Pacific struck him as the bigger challenge. At least Hitler had to contend with Great Britain, and now

Russia, who had entered the war as an Allied Power in June, 1941.

Helen certainly didn't like the idea of Richard going off to war. She was an intelligent young woman who understood why the United States had entered the war, but she wasn't a romantic in the sense that she could enter into the frenzy of watching young men marching off for a noble cause. Richard understood her apprehension, but also knew it was his decision to make. Plus, they both knew they were young, and there would be plenty of time after his return to live out their love.

The bigger problem for Richard was how to tell Lillian and Thomas. Lillian had been surprisingly quiet following their blowup regarding her efforts to make him exempt from the draft. Richard wasn't quite sure how to read the situation. Was she acquiescing, or holding firm on her position?

The following evening was a Friday, and Richard ate very little at dinner. As they were getting up from the table, he asked to have a conversation with them both. They adjoined to the living room where Lillian and Thomas sat down, but Richard remained standing. He came right to the point.

"Mom, I've had a few days to think about what you did for me to keep me exempt from the draft. I know now that you did that out of love, and I appreciate it." Looking at Thomas, he said, "And Dad, I know you haven't said anything to me about it, because you've always wanted me to think things through for myself."

Now, as hard as it was for him to do so, Richard looked straight at his mother and said, "I have been thinking things through. I've spent several afternoons in the library this week, reading about what's going on in the world, and about the commitments the United State has made. I know that Richland is only a tiny speck in this world, but I also know two boys from my high school class who have already enlisted. If they have the courage, why shouldn't I? Their lives are just as important as mine."

Lillian cut in. "Richard, you just said why. You referred to your classmates who enlisted as boys, and they are. And not to be confrontational, but so are you. Please, Richard, don't do anything rash. Go back to Northwestern and finish out the school year, and by that time you'll be in a better position to make a decision."

"Mom, I feel strongly about this and feel the Marine Corps is where I belong."

A look of fear crossed Lillian's face as she clasped her hands over her chest. Thomas looked at his son and tried to offer an affirming smile, but he wasn't quite successful. No one said anything for a good ninety seconds.

Then Lillian said in a tone of meekness Richard had never heard, "Oh Richard, I wish you wouldn't. I know this is your decision to make, but I want to tell you something about me that I never told you before. When I was growing up in this house, there was only one person I loved, my brother Arthur. Fortunately you didn't know your grandparents, but if you did, you'd understand why Arthur and I only had each other. It was always that way between us. When he died of influenza at age fourteen, I didn't think I'd ever be the same again. Your dad and I have a good marriage, but it was when you came into this world, that I felt that same kind of love I had for Arthur. It's selfish of me, but I don't know if I could survive losing you."

Richard was deeply moved. He had always known his mother loved him, but he could never remember her telling him so. It wasn't in her nature to talk about love. It also wasn't her nature to talk about her own vulnerability, so in sharing what it had meant to lose Arthur and what it would mean if anything happened to him laid her heart wide open.

Richard felt choked up. When he found his voice, he responded, "Mom, I'm so deeply touched; I really don't know what to say." He then got up and left the room.

Thomas followed him out and into the entrance foyer. When he caught up with him, he said, "Son, I'm not going to try telling you what to do; I doubt if I could. But even though it was forty years ago, I remember Arthur's funeral like it was yesterday. His coffin was laid out in this hall, and your mother was standing right about where we're standing now. I haven't seen her so distraught...until today. What I'm trying to tell you is, be easy on her."

Richard simply said, "Thanks, Dad," and then, in order to be alone, left the house. The fact was, he had not only made up his mind, but he had already enlisted. He was just trying to get his mother used to the idea before he sprang it on her. He already had his orders to leave for Camp Lejeune in ten days. Not only that, he had made another decision that would further rattle his mother.

Chapter Five: Lillian Has an Attack

He was to meet Helen when she got off work at 8:00 p.m. She already knew about his enlistment.

As they were driving in the country, and ironically as they were passing by two adjacent farms that Lillian owned, Richard said, "Helen, I want you to marry me." She looked at him with an expression of surprise.

Richard continued, "I know I want to spend my life with you, and I think you want to do the same with me. We've talked about holding off that decision until after I come back, but now I realize it would make more sense if we were to go to the Justice of the Peace next week and get married before I report for duty.

That way, you would get regular checks while I'm gone, and things would be easier on you financially. And I don't mean to be morbid, but I bet you'd be entitled to survivor benefits if something were to happen to me. More importantly, if we were married, and you were my widow, Mom would eventually want to take care of you in a generous way. I know her well enough to know that would be the case."

Helen finally responded, "I've only had two days to get used to the idea that you've enlisted. Please, I don't want to hear any talk about being your widow." She paused for a second, and looking at Richard lovingly, "And yes, of course, I do want to spend the rest of my life with you. But running to the Benton court house and being married in a couple of days is a little overwhelming. Can you let me think about it, at least overnight?"

Richard replied, "Fair enough. And that will give me time to buy you a ring. It won't be one of the family heirlooms. From what I know about my ancestors, I wouldn't want their jewelry to touch your finger. Instead, it will represent my love for you, and how much I want you to be in my life forever."

When Richard was returning home and got within a block, he spotted both an ambulance and the doctor's car. A state of panic came over him, and upon arriving, he immediately rushed inside and up to the second floor, where he found his father and his sister sitting outside his mother's room. In an anxious voice, he asked, "What's happened?"

Thomas said, "Your mom's had a heart attack. The doctor wants her to go to the hospital, but you know your mom; she's going to do what she wants, and for now that's to stay in her room. The doctor won't let any of us be with her, but he did allow Marie and me in just long enough to give a smile. I'm sure he'll allow the same for you. I know she'd really appreciate that."

Richard stepped in and made eye contact with Lillian. He offered a smile that said more of his concern than any words could have. He then left and rejoined his dad and sister.

Thomas said to both of them, "Your mother probably never told you because she didn't like to think about her mother, but Irene had heart problems. In fact, that's what took her at a very young age.

Lillian will hate the idea that she is probably inheriting this condition from her mother."

An image suddenly flashed into Richard's mind from earlier in the evening, when he had told his parents about his strong desire to enlist, but had kept from them the fact he already had. Lillian's immediate reaction was to clasp her hands over her chest. Was she having some kind of attack right then? The thought paralyzed him.

What was he to do? He couldn't unenlist...and he didn't want to. He may have been a boy when he graduated from high school the previous May, but he was a man now. The chaos in the world awakened him to a new existence. He was no longer living a life of partial engagement, the life he had lived through all his school years, where he was present only up to a point. He had now shattered through that aloofness and discovered what it meant to be alive.

It wasn't just the state of the world that had rocked him loose from his artificial anchors. Helen turned him in that direction as soon as they started dating. She was real and had invited him to be real. She had prepped him for who he was now becoming.

The following day, when he shared with Helen what had happened with his mom, he reflected, "I don't think I can tell her that we're getting married next week. It would be putting too much on her."

Helen responded, "Of course, we can't be getting married now. I absolutely refuse to consider it. What you have to do is break the news about your enlistment as gently as possible and hope for the best. She's your mother, Richard. Most people in this community know very little about her, and what they think they know is probably wrong. But I do know this. I think you're probably very much like her, and I know that she must love you very much for you to love her back as much as you do."

Richard gave Helen a curious look and was about to respond, when she continued, "Oh, yes. You don't talk about your feelings for your mother, but I know you love her. And that's one of the reasons why I love you so much."

The days ticked away. One morning, he waited until Thomas had finished breakfast and then said, "Dad, we need to talk."

In his perpetual calm voice, Thomas asked, "Have you made your decision?"

In a nervous fashion, Richard answered, "That's just it. I had already made my decision last week. In fact, I had already enlisted in the Marines. I was trying to give Mom a few days to prepare for it. Now I'm nervous as hell about telling her. I'm afraid it might kill her. But I have to leave for Camp Lejeune, in North Carolina in two days."

Thomas, looking at his son, said, "You know you're the one who has to tell her. She's better this morning. She actually had a good breakfast considering what they're allowing her to eat. My advice for you is to tell her this morning. It will be better for her. And knowing we still have two days to be with you will soften the blow."

Then Thomas added, "Son, it will also be better for you. I can see this thing is eating you alive. Let's have some peace in these final days."

Richard needed to brace himself for the task at hand. He went out the kitchen door, walked to the back of their property, and through the gate. He only had to cross the street to enter into the town park which had been named after his great-great-grandfather. Seeing that family name on the arch overhead made him all the more certain of his decision to enlist; he finally needed to feel one with the community and not a fourth-generation overseer. This confidence gave him courage, and after circling the park twice, he returned home.

He went up to his mother's room, and after knocking, entered. Lillian was propped up on some pillows, and she had a peaceful look on her face. Richard was glad she appeared to be in a good place, but hated the idea that what he was about to say would disrupt her tranquility.

He said, "Mom, you look like you're feeling better. Are you?"

"Yes, Richard. A lot better than a few days ago."

"I'm glad," he uttered feebly, as he was losing his courage to share his decision.

Lillian looked into his eyes and said, "Let me make this easier for you. You've come to tell me that you're going to enlist. Don't you think I know you well enough that once you're convinced an action's the right thing to do, nothing is going to dissuade you? You and I are a lot alike. I know you because I know me."

Richard's face was showered with relief. "Mom, yes, you're right." And then, after a moment's hesitation, he continued, "But please forgive me that when I told you that I was thinking about enlisting, I already had. At the time I thought that deception might buy you a few days to get used to the idea."

Lillian tried not to reveal the fresh wave of anxiety coming over her. She asked, "How much longer will I have you home?"

"I have to leave the day after tomorrow." I'll be taking the train to Camp Lejeune, North Carolina, at four on Saturday afternoon."

"Richard, I'm only going to say this once. With every fiber of my body, I wish you wouldn't go. But, also, with every fiber, I couldn't be more proud to have you as my son."

Richard bent down, and doing something he had never done before, kissed his mother on the check.

After he left his mother's room, he called Helen and she was as relieved as he that Lillian had taken the news so well. They both decided that it would be best if he spent his last full day at home, and this meant that what time remaining for them would be in the next few hours.

Fortunately, Helen was free at 1:00 p.m. And after picking her up, he said, "Helen, I'm sure there are thousands of guys this very day trying to talk a woman into having sex, telling her he's off to war and that's how she could send him off. But that's not our case. We'd be married if my mom didn't have a heart attack, and in our minds, we're already married. Let's finally celebrate and make love with no restraint. No more backseat of the car. Let's go to a motel in Watseka and give our love the dignity it deserves." Helen's accepting smile was the only confirmation he needed.

After checking in, there was little inhibition about undressing before each other and making love for the next three hours. The freedom of finally being totally nude, the freedom of allowing their passions to guide them without limit, the freedom of knowing that everything they were doing was right, transported them to a sacred realm neither could have ever anticipated. They were married as much as any couple in the world had ever been married.

Other than a few phone calls, the exchange of a few letters was the only communication Lillian and Thomas had with Richard during his training. Then nine weeks later, they received a telegram informing them that he was to deploy from San Francisco that day. There was certainly no mention as to where. The saying, "Loose lips sink ships," was already becoming a common phrase throughout the country.

Lillian willed herself to become physically stronger, and as the weeks passed she returned to her disciplined work regimen. There were farms, warehouses, and radio stations to manage. She didn't do all this by herself. Dorothy Ziegler, a woman ten years younger, had already been working as her secretary at the house for the past six years. Regarding those who worked for her at a distance, Lillian had an uncanny ability to hire people who were hard-working and honest. She was generous in return.

Her life returned to normal, as normal as possible with Richard fighting in a war. Then, two months later, Marie had an announcement that rocked Lillian's world again. She was pregnant.

To her classmates, the news wasn't so surprising. Marie didn't have a good reputation since her first date at age sixteen. She had always been hungry for love; and subsequently, several boys had discovered that for themselves. Now, particularly tragic, the prospective father was unarguably the most worthless kid in the school.

His name was Dwight Wilson. His dad worked for Thomas at the elevator, and his mother cleaned houses. Dwight was their only child, and not only did he allow his parents to indulge him, he demanded it. He was probably of average intelligence but consistently received low grades as he viewed students who studied as chumps. He was also average in appearance, with auburn hair and blue eyes. However, he did possess an athletic body and was the tallest guy in his class, yet he refused to join the basketball team. From his perspective, there was nothing in it for him.

In fact, that was his perspective about everything. Whereas other guys dated Marie to satisfy their sex drives, Dwight had a much bigger plan. The other guys had used condoms; Dwight refused, telling her that, he "loved her more that way."

When a terrified Marie told Dwight she was pregnant, he assured her, "Don't worry, my love, we'll get married right away, and I'll take care of you."

After a couple of days, Marie asked, "Where will we live?"

Dwight replied, "I'm afraid that my parent's house is so little; we'll have to move in with your folks for the time being."

Marie was panicky at the thought of telling her parents. She declared in anguish, "Dwight, I don't know how I'm going to tell them. Will you come with me?"

Dwight, too big of a coward for that confrontation, replied, "I don't think so, dear. It might be easier on them if they got used to the idea before they met me."

Marie was left to this difficult task on her own. She went first to her dad. Thomas offered these comforting words, "Your baby will be welcomed as any new baby, deserving of all the opportunities this world can offer. I'll be a proud grandpa."

Lillian wasn't quite as gracious. Her abrupt response was, "Give me some time to get used to the idea." But Lillian immediately realized that she had never really loved her daughter as she should, and here was her chance to support her. So Lillian did her best to make Marie feel comfortable with her predicament, and in no time the young couple was married by the Justice of the Peace in Benton. Lillian agreed that they could stay at the Jewell House until they found other quarters.

Dwight had no intention of looking for other quarters. As far as he was concerned, he was finally home, in the biggest and richest house in town. A few months after they had moved in, Marie got up the nerve to ask, "Dwight, don't you think you should be looking for a job of some kind?"

He responded, "What do you have in mind? Pump gas or work at the grain elevator? We're the richest family in town. As a family, we have an image to uphold."

Marie countered, "But Dwight, my dad goes to work at that elevator every day. Why shouldn't you?"

"Because I say so, that's why!"

The question as to how Dwight was to be occupied appeared answered when he got a notice from the local draft board. He had no intention of fighting in a war; only a chump would do that. Like everyone else in town, he knew about Lillian's efforts to keep Richard exempt from the draft, and Dwight's first response was to tell Marie to talk to her mother and get her to do the same for him.

Marie replied with an attitude he wasn't used to hearing, "If you want Mom to intercede on your behalf, you're going to have to ask her yourself."

With a smirk, he countered, "Okay, I will. I'm not afraid of the big bad wolf."

Dwight found Lillian sitting in the music room. He said, "Mother Thorton, there's something I'd like to discuss with you."

Lillian responded, "I would prefer you call me Mrs. Thorton."

Nothing could discourage Dwight's boldness when acting on his own behalf. He continued, "Mrs. Thorton, I want you to prevent me from being drafted like you attempted to do for Richard. It's too bad that he chose to go off to war, but I'm sure you wouldn't want anything to happen to the expectant father of your grandchild."

Lillian's response was immediate. "I'm willing to take that chance."

Dwight, face fell, and then he replied, "Maybe you should take some time to think this over."

Lillian said tersely, "That won't be necessary."

Before he knew what was happening Dwight was drafted, and had no choice but to report to the induction station in Indianapolis. To his immense relief, a heart murmur was discovered and he was sent home. No one was glad to see him.

Now that he was home, Marie once again brought up the subject of Dwight looking for work. He refused to talk about it. In exasperation, Marie said accusingly, "You just married me because my family has money."

Dwight curtly spewed, "What gave you the first clue?"

A few weeks later, Lillian was sitting in the music room. Arthur had told her that he'd always be with her, and when she sat quietly near the piano, she felt his presence. There was a mural of angels painted on the ceiling, and this added to the ambiance that his spirit was near.

Returning to the upstairs, and passing through the entrance foyer, she heard a knock on the door. It was the local boy who delivered Western Union telegrams. From the War Department, it read, "We regret to inform you that Private Richard Thorton was killed in action on August 18, 1942."

Lillian was never the same again.

Chapter Six: Helen's Life Changes

Thirteen years had passed, and it was the spring of 1955. Helen still worked at the Post House but was now the manager. Her plans to enroll at Saint Elizabeth's nursing school never materialized as she had a more pressing challenge. She had been raising a daughter as a single mother.

At first people were eager to believe that Richard Thorton had been the father, but the arithmetic didn't add up. Based on people's memories, it seemed he had left a year or more before the child was born.

But then the gossips theorized the couple had met someplace secretly while he was still in training. What they really wanted to know was the exact date he deployed from San Francisco.

The private business of the Jewell House had always remained private. But now there was an inside mole named Dwight Wilson. He was more than happy to leak information that would make Helen look like a slut. While they were in school together, Helen had always seemed oblivious of Dwight, an unforgivable slight as far as he was concerned.

Armed with this more specific information, gossips had to give up on the theory that Richard was the father, unless a pregnancy could last thirteen months. So, the new theory was that after Richard went off to war, Helen had gone a bit crazy, and apparently some guy passing through the bus station decided that staying a few hours longer would be worth his while. The long and short of it was that no one knew who the father was.

When people got up the nerve to ask, even people in her own family, she always answered the question with another question, "How can I expect others to keep my secret if I can't keep it myself?" In time, people accepted the reality that their curiosity would not be satisfied.

Helen was not beautiful, but she was attractive, and at age thirty-one she did not slip into early matronly status as some women her age did. However, as the years passed, there never seemed to be any men in her life. This, despite the fact that there were a number of local guys who would have been willing to step in and assume the role of a father, with no questions asked. It wasn't just her looks that attracted them; she was so consistently pleasant, and one felt that all their problems disappeared just being in her presence.

Helen had been able to buy a small home in Richland located several blocks from the Jewell House. Built in the 1920s, it was one story with a very simple layout. There was a kitchen and an adjoining nook that opened into the living room. There were also two small bedrooms with a bathroom located at the end of the short hall. An extra, which one might not expect in their simple abode, was the used upright piano situated in the living room.

Her daughter, Judy, was the bright spot in Helen's life, and she had bought the house so that Judy would feel like she was growing up in a proper home...even if there was no father. At a young age, Judy asked her mother why she didn't have a father. Helen had always known that this question would come, yet she felt ripples of anxiety as she did her best to answer. She explained, "Judy, dear, some little girls aren't lucky enough to have both a mother and a father. But I'll do everything in my power to make you feel safe and loved and see that you are well taken care of." The expression on Judy's face communicated that she wasn't quite satisfied, but she did know that her mother loved her and would take good care of her; there was no question about that.

At age twelve, Judy had learned from other girls how babies were made and now realized she had had a father. She very badly wanted to revisit the subject, but also sensed that it would be a painful conversation for her mother. She loved her mother dearly and didn't want to hurt her.

But then a nasty boy by the name of Ronnie Wilson called her a bastard on the playground, and she could tell by everyone's reaction that something horrible had just happened. She asked her best friend, Linda, why being called a bastard was such a bad thing. Linda was torn, she didn't want to be the one to explain it to Judy, but as her friend was compelled do so.

 "Judy, a bastard is someone who is born without their parents being married." She didn't have to say anymore. Judy had never known her father and only recently began to understand that she must have had one.

She was hurt that Ronnie hurled that insult at her in front of all the kids on the playground. Why was he so hateful? True, she had never particularly liked Ronnie. No one else did either, but she had always treated him civilly.

Later that evening, when Helen returned from work, the sting of Ronnie's taunt prompted Judy to find the nerve to ask again about her father. Helen remained silent at first; her face displayed a frozen state that could hide only for a few seconds her distraught emotions. She said, "If anyone has a right to know the answer, it's you. But, honey, I just can't talk about it right now." Then Helen broke into tears and Judy found herself crying as well. She went to her mom and they hugged each other for a long time. No more words were spoken.

Living in a small town, Helen realized that everyone knew everyone and had for generations. She realized that they all knew she was a single mom with no father in sight, and she knew that in some people's eyes, her name should be Jezebel and that their sons shouldn't be seen walking by her house. For these people, she saw that the problem was theirs, that by their harsh judgement, they were inviting a kind of poison into their bloodstream. She also theorized that most people understood that they, too, hadn't lived perfect lives, and were too busy trying to run their own to be giving much thought to hers.

Judy was really hurt by the discovery she was thought of as a bastard, and her pain was Helen's as well. She knew that at age twelve, kids were so sensitive, and Helen feared that Judy was seeing staring eyes every place she went.

Judy did feel that way. Initially she thought there wasn't anything she could do about it, but then decided there was. She could lead the most exemplary life possible. She'd show those people!

Helen and Judy didn't discuss the situation further; Helen just couldn't. But she sensed what her daughter was thinking, that she was going to have to be absolutely perfect from this point forward. Helen was truly stymied. How do you tell your daughter that she didn't really need to be that good?

Judy had always been a good student and up until now, she had breezed through her homework. Now she spent hours every night, and by the following day, she knew more than the teacher.

When she wasn't studying, she was practicing the piano. She had been taking lessons from Mrs. Cook, a local lady that lived in a trailer. Helen knew she'd soon be getting a call from Mrs. Cook, telling her that Judy was beyond the point that there was anything left that she could teach.

Judy's transition into high school was just as significant as if she were leaving one school and entering another. Of course, that wasn't the case in Richland as it was all in the same building. But the younger kids now looked at her as practically an adult, and the older kids were seeing her more as a peer.

Judy was striking. At 5' 7", there were few girls in school taller. She had always been blonde, and by this age, it appeared that it would remain that way. Her eyes were either blue or gray, depending on what she was wearing, and her face was full in a pleasing way, as was her quickly maturing body. In a small town high school, there were only a few lookers in any given class, and Judy was one of them.

Of course, Judy was aware of the effect she had on people, particularly boys; that had actually started around the fifth grade. But now she took notice back. Some of those boys who definitely looked like boys in the fifth grade were now taller, and filling out with definition to their chest. They were developing bigger muscles to their shoulders, arms, and legs, and seemingly out of nowhere, a lower voice arrived that could sound seductive.

Linda had been Judy's best friend since they first started school. Like Judy, she was a town kid. Her dad worked at the local farm implement store, and her mom stayed home to corral her two younger brothers. Linda wasn't another "looker" in their class, but she was the other smart girl. That was pretty much her identity. She wore glasses, but that's not what made her look ordinary. It was more an attitude that suggested that being smart was all she had going for her, so why bother with all the boy/girl stuff. But the truth was, if she would lose the defensive attitude and relax the features in her face, people would discover how attractive she really was.

Judy was involved in various afterschool activities. The most obvious was her role as a cheerleader. Obvious, because being out in front of everyone, she had made up her mind that she wasn't going to hide from those who were judging her.

Helen attended some games to watch her daughter cheer. She hadn't been in that gym since the last game Richard Thorton had played. High on the wall in front of the court was a banner that pronounced, "It doesn't matter if you win or lose, but how you play the game." She had wondered at the sincerity of that sentiment back in her school days, and she wondered about it now.

Judy still needed Helen as a mother, but in different ways. Clearly she didn't need as much of her time.

Since she was the manager at the Post House she considered putting herself down for more hours. But that wouldn't be fair to those already working those hours. She had been treated well from the very start and wanted to do the same for others.

She even thought about arranging her schedule so that she could finally take some nursing classes in Lafayette. She discovered that the only kind of classes she could take, short of a nursing degree, was to prepare as a nursing assistant. A nursing assistant would do the challenging work of bathing patients, changing patients, turning patients, and cleaning up messes of every kind. It wasn't that Helen wasn't willing to do that kind of work. In fact, the necessity of it appealed to her. But she couldn't make the kind of money that she was earning at the Post House, and needed that cash flow as long as she was raising Judy.

The whole question was answered when a man came into her life. His name was Vernon Haley and he had been in Newton less than a week before they connected on each other. He worked in the research department of a seed corn processing plant that was located almost next door, and he had come over to grab a quick lunch. Vernon was from Tennessee, and his smile was as slow as his drawl. Helen found both engaging.

Chapter Seven: Demon Child

Much had also happened in Lillian's life during the years Judy Bennett was growing up. Thomas had a stroke in September, 1945, and passed away a week later. Throughout their marriage, he had repeatedly told Lillian that he loved her, but Lillian could never say those words back. Still, Thomas always knew. In his last few days, having lost his ability to speak, his declaration of love was fervently expressed with his eyes.

Lillian was devastated. Through the years, she knew she counted on Thomas a great deal, but hadn't realized how much. He had been her rock; the only one she had ever known.

People assumed that he would be buried in the Henry lot at the cemetery south of town. Edward Henry had been Lillian's, great-grandfather, the illustrious land baron of the previous century. He had arranged for a life-sized statue to be erected as his memorial. It was placed on a twelve foot pedestal because it was said he wanted to be high enough to gaze at all the land he owned.

Lillian decided to make other arrangements. She hurriedly bought plots a distance away that would be for the Thorton family. Thomas had been more the head of a family than she could have ever hoped, and she ordered a large headstone erected to signify that fact.

Lillian had so badly wished that Richard's body could be brought home, but the War Department stated that that wasn't a possibility. Lillian understood that to mean there had been too little left of him to positively identify. She had also learned that the day he was killed was very early in the Battle of Guadalcanal. When Lillian went to her encyclopedia to read about Guadalcanal, it was described as a speck in the Solomon Islands.

This description immobilized her. She recalled Richard making his case why he needed to fight in the war. She remembered his exact words, "I know that Richland is only a little speck in this world, but I also know two boys from my high school class have already enlisted. If they have the courage, why shouldn't I? Their lives are just as important as mine."

Lillian continued her reflection, "So, Richard went from one tiny little speck in the world to another, and gave up his life.

He had been the first fatality of the war from Richland. They had always been the first family of the town, and they were first once again. Lillian felt the bitter irony.

Lillian suffered another loss two years after Thomas died. Dwight and Marie were coming home from a night out in Lafayette when Dwight lost control of their car and smashed into a telephone pole. Both were killed instantly. Dwight had been drinking; he had been doing a lot of that lately. He had also been quite nasty when anyone tried to intervene.

One of his former classmates, who had never liked Dwight, heard the news while having a beer at the local bar. He reflected on Dwight's mantra, "what's in it for me," and wondered if Dwight realized in his final seconds that the telephone pole was "what was in it for him."

Both Marie and Dwight were buried in the Thorton plot. Lillian had perceived Dwight as odious from the beginning, and her judgement was re-confirmed with each passing year. But he was the father of Marie's son, and for that reason alone, Marie would have wanted him buried with respect.

Lillian knew she had failed Marie. Had she been able to love her as she had loved Richard, Marie would have been a much different person. She wouldn't have been riddled with the insecurities that led her into a marriage with someone as worthless as Dwight.

With Thomas and both her children taken from her, she poured herself into her work. The war years were good for farmers, so her landholdings were yielding impressive profits. She decided to sell off her California warehouses at a huge profit and expanded her radio broadcast holdings in the Midwest. She purchased WILL in Champaign, Illinois, WROK in Rockford, Illinois, and WJOB in Hammond, Indiana.

In addition to her charitable giving to the urban poor, and the American Red Cross, Lillian gave generously to the American Stroke Foundation. She also found a charity she thought might help her better accept Richard's death, the Hiroshima Peace Centre Foundation. It helped pay for reconstructive surgery for people disfigured by the A-bomb. Lillian didn't want bitterness to add to her pain of loss.

So many people around the world had suffered.

Over the years, Lillian had made many changes to Jewell House. Almost as soon as her father was given his walking papers, amenities such as electricity and indoor plumbing were installed. She also commissioned a major redo of the master bedroom suite, wanting nothing to remind her of her mother. Irene had required a sizable dressing room, lined with mirrors. Now that space became a very functional office. A few years later, the carriage house was converted into a garage.

When the white wicker furniture on the front porch and the garden chair in back wore out, Lillian ordered that they be replaced with exact duplications. Both returned her to memories of Arthur.

The rest of the house held little sentimental value. The kitchen had been remodeled several times, making it easier for the staff to function. Unlike her mother, she never referred to the staff as "servants" or "maids." She found those words demeaning.

The living room was large and oblong. The north wall had a fireplace at its center and doors to each side. One led into the dining room, the other into the breakfast room. The wall opposite seemed more like a furniture store display, with sofas and chairs all lined up next to each other. The living room had never been much in use. Irene and Cyrus had stayed to their rooms, Lillian and Arthur had preferred being outside or in the music room; and Richard and Marie found little use for the room, preferring to listen to the smaller radio in the breakfast room. It was an unfriendly room, but then the whole house was built to be unfriendly. It was built to say, "Look what I have and you don't."

At this point, the biggest challenge in Lillian's life was her grandson, Ronnie, who was born less than three months after Richard was killed. Originally, there was talk of naming him Richard, but Lillian suspected correctly that this was another ploy of Dwight's to score points. Lillian explained to Marie that hearing Richard's name would be too painful. Dwight's next choice was to call him his own middle name, Ronald, and from the very beginning the child was called Ronnie.

Ronnie wasn't quite five when his parents were killed. He had known a mother who spent time with him and showed him kindness. His dad didn't really seem to care. But at the same time, Ronnie had the uncanny ability to sense that even though it was his mother's family who was important, it was his dad who controlled his mother. A template had been set; he wanted to be like his father.

Of immediate concern to Lillian: who was going to care for the child? Dwight's mother had serious health issues, so that was not an option. Besides, Lillian felt that it would be a betrayal to Marie not to do her best for the child. If only Thomas was still alive. It was he more than Lillian who had raised their children on a practical, day-by-day basis.

Ronnie was too young for school, and Richland had no kindergarten program. Even though the days of children being tutored at home were long gone, Lillian felt, for the present, that the best solution would be to have someone with the child who could form his character rather than just babysit him. With that in mind, she asked her secretary to look into recently retired teachers who might want some added income.

Dorothy contacted the principal, Mr. Coffee, and he recommended Miss Ida Hook. Ida had taught various elementary classes in her twenty-seven year career. She and her sister Genevieve, lived in a house next to the school; the lot adjoined land that their father had owned and farmed. Ida was a petite woman but never had disciplinary problems. Mr. Coffee remembered Dwight, and if Ronnie was anything like the father, a teacher who knew how to maintain discipline would be much appreciated. Ida was hired.

Part of Ida's method of maintaining discipline was never to smile. She had always felt that a smile on her face would open the door for a rambunctious kid to act out.

It was also her practice to keep her students busy. So even though Ronnie could neither read nor write, he could learn to write his letters. She had him doing this endlessly. Only when she felt she had him totally under her thumb, would he be allowed to go outside and play in the garden. But even during these respites, she was watching him like a hawk. Ida appeared to be holding the upperhand. That was until the day when Ronnie, with his head down, charged at her, knocked her to the ground, and came close to biting off the tip of her nose.

Mr. Coffee's next recommendation was Mr. Bronson, a retired coach and science teacher. He had had no experience with a pupil that young, but what he did bring to the job was bulk. He was six-foot, and because he had never quit doing pushups and sit-ups, his two-hundred-pound body was still fairly taut.

Mr. Bronson took a different approach. He and Ronnie often took long walks...as far as Ronnie's five-year-old legs could carry him. There was a little creek just outside of town called Sugar Creek, and Mr. Bronson had much to share with Ronnie about the tadpoles, frogs, and the little fish. He also told Ronnie about the wildflowers that grew, and how the Indians that had lived in the area a hundred years earlier would use those flowers as medicine. It appeared that Mr. Bronson was the right person for the job. Then one day while Mr. Bronson was sitting along the creek, Ronnie got up behind the older man, found the biggest rock his spindly little body could lift, and smashed it at the back of his head. Mr. Bronson was dazed, but didn't pass out. However, when he got Ronnie home he made it clear that he would not be returning.

At this point, Lillian realized it was pointless to go back to Mr. Coffee. Who in God's name would be willing to take on Ronnie? Then Dorothy came up with an idea. There was a divorcee in town, Trudy Travis, who made a meager living sitting for the elderly and also babysitting children. Dorothy suspected that she would be willing to take on Ronnie if the pay was right.

At this point, Lillian was far beyond looking for someone who could shape Ronnie's character. Her goal now was to find someone who could contain him and keep him occupied until he entered school.

And more than anything, she wanted someone who could keep Ronnie as far from her as possible. With each passing year, he looked more and more like his father. He didn't have Dwight's auburn hair or blue eyes. Ronnie's hair and eyes were brown. But nevertheless, he had his father's smirk and the same fat lower lip, that, when pushed out, spoke of insolence.

Trudy Travis was invited over and she jumped at the chance. She would be in the biggest house with the richest family in town.

Her manner of managing Ronnie was quite different from either Ida Hook's or Mr. Bronson's. She pretty much let him do whatever he wanted. This worked well for the first three weeks. But like anyone caring for young children, she was always relieved to put the child to bed successfully. On one particular night, he raised his hand in the air as if he wanted to touch her cheek. The gesture surprised Trudy, and she saw it as a sign of how far she had won him over.

Instead, with all his might, Ronnie slapped her across the face. Startled but undaunted, she slapped him right back. He in turn slapped her again. She responded by pulling her hand back as far as she could and slapping him with a wallop that would have rattled an adult. Ronnie didn't cry; he'd never show that sign of weakness. But he had met his match. They understood each other.

After Ronnie started school, Trudy was retained to watch him after school and be with him until bedtime. Ronnie didn't have any friends so it was just the two of them, and the years passed. He was in the same class as Judy Bennett, and it was Trudy that told Ronnie that Judy was a bastard.

Transitioning into high school didn't change Ronnie's friendless status. For one thing, he was always acting out in class, and he never took any of his studies seriously. He really didn't see why he should. That was because Trudy impressed on him almost daily that Lillian's wealth was his birthright, and with her history of having one heart attack, it was only a matter of time before she kicked.

Regarding Ronnie's potential wealth, Trudy wasn't just acting as a cheerleader; she expected a big cut for herself. She came up with a figure of $40,000 as her payout, and repeated the demand so often that Ronnie eventually accepted the idea.

Trudy grew up in Plato, Missouri. She met Jerry Travers while he was training at nearby Fort Leonard Wood. She was just eighteen-years-old and he twenty when they entered a very passionate relationship. Jerry grew up in Richland, and had little experience in the romance department. What he didn't understand was that Trudy at eighteen had had quite a bit. She was a hot number: red-haired and voluptuous.

When Jerry got his orders to ship to Germany with a combat engineering company, they hurriedly decided to marry. Actually, the decision wasn't so hurried for Trudy; she had made that decision the week after she met Jerry. She had had a miserable childhood and was looking for a ticket out of town: destination anywhere.

Jerry had an earnest quality that communicated he would always take care of her, and more than anything, that's what she wanted. Her parents were both drunks, but managed to hold their factory jobs. Not liking the idea of parenthood, they boarded her with her grandparents. The initial idea was they'd spend time with her on weekends, but in time, the weekend visits evaporated. The grandparents only agreed if they were being paid more for those extra days. She'd alternate between both sets of grandparents who lived on farms. Trudy had no end of chores.

Before Jerry shipped to Germany to aid in post-war construction, he took his bride home to live with his family. Trudy liked the security, but after several months of Richland's quiet life, she became restless. Still not old enough to go to Tom's Tap, the solo venue of nightlife in town, she decided to get cozy with the mechanic who lived across the street.

Trudy's attempts at discretion weren't convincing. She befriended another military bride who lived in town, who, unbeknownst to Trudy, had a horrible reputation. So she was raising a red flag every time she claimed that the two of them had gone to Newton to see a movie.

The mechanic's wife confronted Trudy one day in the presence of Trudy's in-laws. Seems it wasn't the only time the mechanic had strayed, and the whole town knew about it. Jerry's parents were loyal to their son, and gave Trudy a home until he returned. When he did, he booted her out.

Trudy more or less floundered until the position at the Jewell House opened. Now, after spending several years with Ronnie, she was awaiting her payday.

Chapter Eight: Judy

Judy had always been popular with her classmates. She was smart, and being smart, if one isn't obnoxiously smart, can be very attractive. She was also genuinely kind and that, too, made her very attractive. And, of course, she was aware of the way boys looked at her.

Helen gave the green light for Judy to date after her sixteenth birthday. That prospect provoked both excitement and anxiety. Like any teenage girl, Judy was looking forward to the special attention one receives on a date. But, she was anxious because the sting of being called a bastard in the seventh grade left its mark. She was still committed to leading a blameless life, and that meant when a boy pushed for what he wanted, she'd be able to push back harder. She was already hearing which girls in the school were marked as easy. She felt it to be so unfair because the boy's reputations never seemed to suffer any consequences. If anything, they were enhanced.

If she could make her own choice of who to date, it would be Dave Schuster. He had a lot going for him. For one thing, he was good-looking. His dark brown hair was cut in a flat top, and his eyes were an unusual color of teakwood brown. He was 6'1" and was lean in a solid way that one achieves by playing sports all one's life, which indeed he had. He was also the smartest boy in class, and appeared to excel effortlessly in math and science.

Judy saw a lot of Dave as he was also a sophomore and they shared the same classes. Just as Judy shared honors as smartest girl with her best friend Linda, Dave shared the same kind of recognition with his friend, Eugene. Dave and Eugene were quite different in appearance; Dave was over 6' and Eugene was 5'7". They both played on the basketball team, with Dave considered a star. But one advantage of attending a school with a small enrollment; everyone has a chance to make the team, if they're willing to work at it. Eugene worked very hard on a jump shot that he would take whenever he could, and he also managed to draw a number of fouls. He was so good at making foul shots that Richland fans were already counting the points before he shot them.

Dave was a town kid, the youngest of three boys. His dad was Bill and his mother's name was Millie. Bill was quite proud that he built his own business distributing heating oil, a considerable leap from his dad's career of working for Thomas at the elevator. Dave looked like his father, only twenty-five years younger. Bill was still in pretty good shape, except for some softness that had settled around his middle.

When Dave asked Judy out, he expected her to say yes; every girl in his short dating history had. He was actually going to ask her the week before, but then he checked what movies would be playing at the Benton and the Newton (each theater named after the towns in which they were located). It was customary to let the girl make the choice, and "War and Peace" was playing at the Benton and "Moby Dick" at the Newton. Dave didn't want to take a chance that Judy might choose "War and Peace." A friend of his had seen it weeks earlier in Lafayette, and told him it lasted almost three and a half hours. A movie that length, based on an old, Russian novel, sounded like pure torture.

The options for the following weekend were much more inviting. "Love Me Tender" would play in Newton and "The Man Who Knew Too Much" in Benton.

Dave was surprised when Judy chose "The Man Who Knew Too Much." He assumed all girls were gaga over Elvis Presley, and would want to see his first film. In fact, he himself was a big Elvis fan. But he also liked Jimmy Stewart, particularly in a string of Westerns he made earlier in the 50s.

When the movie was over, Dave took Judy to Senesac's Restaurant for a hamburger. Judy had been there countless times, but never on a date, which made this occasion something special.

Dave asked, "Did you like the movie?"

Judy replied, "Yes, I'm a big Alfred Hitchcock fan. Did you see "Rear Window?"

Dave replied with a question, "Is that the one where a guy's in a wheelchair and thinks the guy across the courtyard killed his wife?"

Judy responded enthusiastically, "Yes, it was Jimmy Stewart, the same actor who was in tonight's movie. And there was something else that was the same. Alfred Hitchcock signals to the audience that the hero is in peril before that character realizes it himself. So since the audience identifies with the hero, they're freaking out because, vicariously, they feel in peril."

Dave smiled at Judy in a way she had never seen and exclaimed, "Wow! You're just so darn smart, Judy. Who thinks that much about what's going on in a movie? But I like that you do, and maybe I'll catch on, too."

Judy expounded, "I just don't think about them while I'm watching them. If they're really good, I continue thinking about them, sometimes for days. It's the same with books. Don't you find yourself thinking about the characters as real people and wonder what happens to them after you've read the last page?"

Dave offered that same smile Judy had just seen. He said, "To be honest, I don't think I do. Most books I read are something assigned from class, and I'm just glad to get to the last page." The two talked more about movies they had liked, and Judy even got Dave to discuss books they had read for class.

When Dave took her home, he promptly got out of the car and walked around to open Judy's door. They got to the house and he bent down to give Judy a gentle kiss that seemed so shy that it surprised her. But It was exactly what she had hoped for.

Dave returned to his car and drove away smiling. He always knew he liked Judy; he had his whole life. But had he ever known how special she was? Now, he had a one word summation, "Wow!"

Judy, too, had been quite pleased with her date. She reflected that since they first started school together, she knew he was a good student and liked that about him. And as far back as the fifth grade, before most girls and boys start looking at each other in a new way, she had found him attractive. He had appeared to be "more boy" than the other boys in his class. He was taller the best athlete on the playground. But he only seemed interested in what a boy might be interested.

Tonight she saw a different side of him. He lit up when she had taken the conversation into analyzing movies and books. On those occasions, his smile conveyed that he was seeing her in a new light and was really impressed with her thoughts on those subjects. That, plus the soft kiss by which he had concluded their date revealed a surprising vulnerability.

Judy walked into an empty house. She was getting used to this new reality as her mom was seeing more and more of Vernon Haley. She welcomed the idea of her mom dating; she wanted her to experience anything that could contribute to her happiness.

But were Helen and Vernon actually dating? They were seen dining out in restaurants in Benton and Newton, and now and then, they were spotted at the local movie theaters. But to look at them, they appeared to be more like friends. And for people who would notice, and there were such people, Vernon never seemed to stay at Helen's house long enough for anything romantic to be happening.

Vernon was on the quiet side, so even people who were experts at dragging information out of people were stymied. At work, he calmly focused on the challenges at hand, and his usual reaction to people's gratuitous comments was a quiet smile at most.

Then one day, a fellow worker was recalling his days in the Navy during World War II. He then asked Vernon if he had served.

Vernon answered, "I was in the Navy, too."

"What ship were you on?"

"The Intrepid."

"Wasn't that an aircraft carrier?"

"Yep."

Getting information out of Vernon was like drinking molasses through a straw, but his fellow worker persisted with one more question. "Where did you train?"

"Great Lakes."

When this little bit of information finally reached certain ears, it was enough to start up the rumor mill all over again. Gossiping voices wanted to know: "Why was he the first man Helen was willing to spend time with?" "Why was Vernon Haley in Newton in the first place?" "Why hadn't he married at a younger age?" "Didn't Vernon Haley come from Tennessee? And if he was taking a bus to Great Lakes, wouldn't he have stopped at the Post House in Newton on his way?" "Wasn't Helen Bennett working there from the beginning of the war?" "Isn't it interesting that Judy Bennett has such blonde hair while her mother's hair is so dark. And if you really look at Vernon, he has the color of hair a lot of people have if they were blonde as a child." And lastly, the question, "Would Vernon have been the kind of guy to grab quick sex on the run?" was quickly turned into a statement that declared, "You can't rule out any man when such an opportunity presents itself!" For those who cared about such things, they strongly suspected Vernon was Judy's father and that he had finally come back into Helen's life.

Tom's Tap was a respectable establishment, but not all their patrons were paragons of virtue. Trudy was one of the less reputable, and many nights she left with some guy on the make. The whole town knew this about her, but she couldn't have cared less. In her mind, she was "living," whereas the other denizens of Richland were merely "existing."

Sometimes she would tell Ronnie about her tawdry affairs, and he admired her for thwarting convention. That was the path he had always been on, and he salivated at the thought of how he would live once he got his money.

One night Trudy got into a conversation with a stranger sitting at the bar. His name was Brian Murphy, and he was looking for someone to take a dog off his hands. He and his wife were passing through Richland because that was where she had grown up. He was a military man who had been stationed in Germany, and they were on their way to Japan. While in Germany, he had trained a boxer to be a police dog, but he couldn't take him to

Japan. The dog's name was Ajax. Did Trudy know anyone who might want to take Ajax off his hands? He added, "In all fairness, I have to caution you that Ajax was trained to be a fighter and can be mean."

In her early years with Ronnie, he had wanted a dog, but Trudy knew who would be taking care of it and consistently vetoed the idea. Now he was in high school and old enough to take care of the dog himself. But what she really liked about Ajax was hearing he was mean. She knew Ronnie would like that, too.

Two days later, Ajax was delivered to the Jewell House, and the following day, the Murphys departed for Japan. Ronnie and Ajax took to each other immediately; they shared a kindred spirit of hostility. It took a few more days before Ajax and Trudy became friends, but once the dog understood she was Ronnie's ally that tension passed.

Lillian hadn't been consulted about Ronnie acquiring a dog, but long ago, she adapted the view that anything that occupied the boy and could keep him out of her sight was a good thing. The staff was afraid of the dog, and Ronnie took delight in the idea that he had a new lever of power.

It had been a number of years since Lillian had visited a doctor's office, and Doctor Cotton was scheduled to arrive any minute for a regular checkup. Meanwhile, Lillian and Dorothy were conducting routine business affairs. Lillian had been walking away from her desk when, all of a sudden, she collapsed to the floor, her hands clasped on her chest.

Chapter Nine: Another Attack

Dorothy was quick to place a nitroglycerin tablet under Lillian's tongue just as the doctor was walking into the room. He knelt down next to his patient and asked, "Lillian, can you hear me?"

In a weak voice, she responded, "Yes."

"I have one more medication I want to give you, quinidine that treats irregular rhythms. Then we're going to get you to the hospital."

"I'm not going to the hospital. You can treat me right here."

"I'm afraid, Lillian, I'm going to have to insist. First of all, we can't be sure that what you're experiencing is a heart attack unless we get some imaging. Secondly, we don't know if you need oxygen administered. Being out of breath isn't the only indication that oxygen is needed."

It took twenty minutes for the ambulance to arrive from Newton for the ride to Lafayette. It wasn't exactly an ambulance; it was the same vehicle used as the hearse. But in these small communities, people understood the need to consolidate and were grateful for the accommodation.

At the hospital, it was confirmed that Lillian had had a heart attack and was told her hospital stay would last several days. Meanwhile, Doctor Cotton determined that Lillian would require a caregiver be present around the clock, and this had left him and Dorothy scrambling to create the necessary staffing. Trudy was approached to take the day shift. It had been many years since Ronnie needed a sitter, and she had basically been on the payroll as his paid friend. Trudy accepted; she calculated that closer proximity to Lillian would get her nearer to her big payday. Ruth, the live-in housekeeper for the past ten years, agreed to take the night shift, and her single bed was moved into a corner of Lillian's large room.

That left evenings and weekends. Mrs. Brown, an LPN from Newton, agreed to keep watch on the weekends, and Dr. Cotton thought he had the perfect candidate for the evening shift. He called Helen and asked if he could drop over to visit with both she and Judy that evening.

When he arrived, he immediately got to the point. He had known Judy since his arrival in Richland ten years earlier, and knew that she was a good student and interested in pursuing a nursing career. He thought that being a caretaker for Mrs. Thorton would offer excellent experience. He was sure there would be time for her to do her homework as Mrs. Thorton wasn't a chatty person and would be engaged in her own activities. And on the weekday nights Judy couldn't do it, either Dorothy or Ruth would be willing to fill in. He surmised the pay was pretty good at $4.00 an hour.

He then said, "Judy, I hate to rush you, but we need to have the necessary staffing completed before Mrs. Thorton comes home. Can you give me an answer by tomorrow evening?"

Judy, somewhat overwhelmed by this turn of events, replied, "I think so. Let me talk it over with Mom."

After Dr. Cotton left, Judy asked Helen, "Have you ever met Mrs. Thorton?"

Helen simply stated, "No."

Judy queried, "Isn't it strange that no one ever seems to have met her, and yet she's considered the matriarch of the town. I've accepted that as the way it has always been...but it's so strange."

After a moment of silence that Helen made no effort to break, Judy asked, "What do you think I should do?"

"I'm going to leave the decision entirely to you. It doesn't sound as if your studies would be affected, and that would be my only objection."

The following evening, Judy called Dr. Cotton and accepted the offer.

Her best friend Linda already had an after-school job at Mose Martin's Drugstore. She was in charge of the soda fountain which enjoyed its biggest activity during the three hours after school was dismissed. Both the drugstore and Mose Martin were town institutions. Mose had been at this location prior to the great flu epidemic of 1918 and held a record for being the longest-working pharmacist in the state of Indiana. The décor of the soda fountain and seating for its customers reflected this longevity. Everyone took for granted the marble topped café tables with the copper finished framed chairs because they had always been there.

The building itself had a prior history as Hadley's Hardware Store, going back before the turn of the century. Mose retained the plank flooring and cabinets of that earlier era, and kept them shiny with polishing oil.

If Mose looked out the front window and to the right, he would see Hwy 41 which ran adjacent to Richland. When he had first arrived in town, that national highway had yet to be paved.

If Linda looked out that same window and directly across street, she would see Klemme and Cooley Implement Store where her father worked. Sometimes she liked the idea of him being so close; yet other times it gave her a suffocating feeling like her life would never go anywhere.

Dave didn't have steady work. Sometimes, he'd be hired by Eugene's dad for seasonal work such as baling hay.

More often, he'd help out at the elevator. But there was one thing everyone in town understood: nothing was ever to interfere with his basketball practice and basketball games.

Dave was now unquestionably the star of the team, certainly not a surprise to his peers who had recognized his talent all through their growing-up years. However, that generation probably didn't realize that he was part of a basketball legacy. William, his dad, had been the star of Richland's team in 1934.

For Dave, it was just something he did well. For his dad, basketball was who he was. And though by the time Dave was playing ball, Bill had been in a good marriage, had three sons, and owned his own business, basketball was still who he was. But now he was living it vicariously through his youngest son.

His oldest son Bud (William Junior) knew he was too short to be impressive on the floor and never really tried. He was now working for his dad in the heating oil distribution business and was taking that seriously.

The middle son Bob was tall enough, but just didn't have the athletic ability. He also struggled academically and often got into fights. One time when Dave was nine, and Bob was eleven, Bob practically beat him to a pulp. No one could ever figure out why. They didn't seem to understand what a lifetime of being jealous of a younger brother, who was better looking, a better athlete, and clearly smarter, could do to a kid. Now Bob was in the Army and his parents were hoping the experience would straighten him out.

So, it was up to Dave. He was Bill's last chance at basketball reincarnation.

Dave's mother Millie was a housewife; she was too delicate to work, and Bill wouldn't have wanted her to. From the start, Bill had viewed Millie's fragility as an asset, a delicate flower that he could care for. She and Bill had known each other since their school days, and had been in love for as long. It was a good marriage. Millie had grown up a farm kid, and when her father died, the farm went to her older brother. That was the way it was done, and she hadn't expected anything different.

Her delicacy took on new meaning when she was pregnant with Dave. She suffered from pre-eclampsia, and from then on, she was at risk for cardiovascular disease.

When Lillian arrived home from the hospital, she didn't like the idea of the caregiving staff, but Dr. Cotton had convinced her of its need. She was now seventy-three years old, and longevity wasn't in her genes. Her mother Irene had only reached forty-three, and her father Cyrus passed away at the age of sixty-seven.

Trudy explained to Ronnie why she had accepted a position that would prevent her from spending much time with him. She said, "I hope you understand how this will work out for you. You'll have a spy who can tell you everything your grandmother is up to. I'll be there when she's working with Dorothy, so we'll finally know what all her mysterious business holdings are. I'll be there when the doctor visits, and I'll size up how vulnerable her health really is. And I'll be there when old man Bark comes to discuss her legal affairs."

Ronnie responded, "And you could be talking me up. She doesn't like me much." Then a sense of relish crossed his face, as he continued, "But really, what does it matter? I'm her only heir!"

Ronnie had particular animus toward the lawyer Nathan Bark. He had wanted to buy a Ford Thunderbird convertible, but had saved nothing from the small monthly income he received from his grandfather Thorton's will. So when he called Mr. Bark and told him he wanted a $3,300 advance on his inheritance, Mr.

Bart replied, "Mr. Wilson, you'll have to clear that with your grandmother."

Ronnie shouted into the phone, "I'm not asking her. I'm telling you. Don't you understand that giving me the money will serve your best interests once I get all my money?"

Mr. Bark responded, "I'm sorry, Mr. Wilson. You'll have to talk with Mrs. Thorton."

"Ronnie exclaimed, "You're the one who's going to be sorry!"

When Trudy reported for her first day as caretaker, she started off on the wrong foot. Previously in sitting for the elderly, she had called her clients "Honey," assuming that they found that endearing. The first time she tried that with Lillian, Lillian responded, "People, even people

I've known for many years, address me as Mrs. Thorton. I'd appreciate if you'd do the same."

Trudy thought to herself, "She's really the witch I've always assumed she'd be," but responded quickly, "Yes, Mrs. Thorton. We wouldn't want us to be uncomfortable with each other."

Lillian rejoined just as quickly, "I'd also prefer that you didn't discuss you and me as the collective "us." Trudy had a lost look on her face so Lillian explained. "If you meant to say you didn't want me to feel uncomfortable, then you should have said "you" instead of "us." If you don't feel comfortable, that's your concern."

What Trudy had attempted was a form of baby-talk. She thought it had worked before with her older clients, and it had given her a sense of control. This definitely wasn't going to work with Lillian.

Trudy was able to effectively eavesdrop when Lillian and Dorothy were discussing business affairs, and she didn't like what she was hearing. Apparently, there were charities that Lillian supported. Trudy and Ronnie, both being who they were, never suspected that there could be this kind of drain on Ronnie's money. This particular day, Lillian and Dorothy were discussing a non-profit in Seattle that had expanded Boys Club of America to include girls. The amount of money that Lillian was sending in support left Trudy staggering. She wondered, "How much more of Ronnie's money was his grandmother giving away?"

When Trudy's shift was over, she found Judy waiting in the music room. She said to her, "She is really a BITCH! Honey, she'll eat you alive." With that, she went to the living room where she knew Ronnie would be watching television. He asked, "What did you find out?"

Trudy replied, "She's the tarantula we always knew she'd be. And what's worse, she's busy giving away our money!"

Meanwhile, as Judy was climbing the stairs, she asked herself, "What have I gotten myself into?" But before reaching the second floor, she thought about Trudy Travis and what she knew about her. She decided she'd make up her own mind about Mrs. Thorton.

She knocked on the door and heard a strong voice say, "Come in." The strength of the voice had emanated from character rather than vigor. As she entered the room, Lillian was sitting at her desk and said, "Have a seat; I'll just be a minute."

Lillian knew Judy was Helen's daughter. After Richard was killed, and Lillian had learned Helen had an out-of-wedlock daughter a year after he departed for Camp Lejeune, she took comfort that, at least her judgment had been right about Helen. In fact, she questioned if she wanted her daughter now as a caregiver, but Dorothy vouched for both mother and daughter, "You're really not going to find nicer people in Richland."

Finally, Lillian turned toward Judy and without Judy saying the first word, she knew Dorothy's assessment had been right. Judy smiled and looked at Lillian with directness. It was the kind of look one gives when they really want to know someone and are willing to make the effort to do so. Plus, Judy was quite pretty; for some reason Lillian hadn't expected that.

She asked, "Tell me about you, Miss Bennett."

Judy replied, "I'm a junior in high school. I live on Oak Street with my mother, Helen Bennett; I don't remember living in any other house other than that one."

"Do you like school, Judy?"

"Yes, I always have. I've liked everything about it."

"And what do you want to do after high school?"

"I think I want to be a nurse. But I'm not sure and am glad to have another year to think about it."

Lillian asked, "Did you bring any of your schoolbooks with you?"

"Yes, I left them downstairs."

"Then why don't you get them, and do your homework while I finish up a few more things at my desk."

Judy said, "Thank you. That's very thoughtful of you." As she went to retrieve her books, she thought, "What was Trudy Travis talking about? Mrs. Thorton is nice. I'm not sure why that comes as such a big surprise, but it does."

The housekeeper brought up trays of supper for both of them. That was another surprise. The rest of the evening remained quiet.

When Judy went down to leave, Ronnie met her in the entrance foyer with Ajax in tow. He said menacingly, "Just remember whose house you're in."

Judy responded with a look that conveyed, "Ronnie, you're not making any sense, but then you never do."

Chapter Ten: Ronnie to the Rescue

Judy very much enjoyed the time she spent with Lillian, and one year followed into the next. Her admiration for the woman's intelligence continued to increase, and she deeply respected Lillian's philanthropic endeavors. It struck her as impressive that so much good could be generated for so many from a solitary house in the little town of Richland.

Judy also found Lillian's business affairs fascinating, particularly the six television stations she had acquired in addition to her radio holdings. Lillian received more than one trade journal that listed weekly ratings, and Judy enjoyed perusing the lists. "Gunsmoke" was almost always rated number one.

Judy didn't watch a lot of television; she was too occupied with school work, cheerleading, and spending time with Dave. The exception was "The Loretta Young Show" which aired on Sunday night. She wanted to see what glamourous star wore as she swept through the door to introduce that night's story. "The Loretta Young Show" never made the Top 10, but it held its own, regardless what the competition threw against it.

Sometimes, after Dorothy left for the day, Lillian would want to know certain stock values listed in the "Wall Street Journal." Judy would read them for her, and in doing so, developed an interest in certain stocks she began to follow for herself.

Because of her farm holdings, Lillian also had a keen interest in the futures' market and Judy assisted her in following certain commodities. Judy quickly learned about the "why and the how" of the futures' market. Judy had taken the school's General Business Course the semester before, but she was learning so much more from Lillian.

Judy and Dave dated each other exclusively, but they didn't consider themselves "going steady" as some couples did. That is, they didn't engage in the ritual by which the boy would give his class ring to the girl, and she in turn would wear it on a chain around her neck, wrapped in angora wool.

Judy and Dave felt just as serious about each other as these other couples, maybe more so. But they knew they had a long future ahead of them before they could marry. For Judy, it would be three years of nursing school.

For Dave, he saw an eternity of wait. That's because his father expected him to become a doctor. Early on, his dad determined there had to be some good reason why Dave was so gifted in the sciences.

Plus, maybe if he was a doctor, Millie might receive the optimal treatment for her heart condition. When Dave was still in grade school, his older brother Bud told him that their mom wouldn't be suffering from heart illness had she not had difficulty giving birth to him.

Dave would need to complete undergraduate work, and then medical school. But to compound the situation, what money his father had in savings was being held in reserve for medical emergencies Millie might require. So Bill's plan for Dave was that he should first enlist in the Army for four years and qualify for the GI Bill. From his dad's point of view, the GI Bill would offer the perfect solution. But as eighteen-year-old Dave saw it, he'd be held captive for the next fourteen years of his life.

Trying not to think about it, he focused on academics, playing basketball, and Judy. Really, Judy came first on that list. He was in love with her, and in love with all the intensity an eighteen-year-old boy could feel. Their lovemaking had evolved a long way from the shy kiss of their first date. He now desired to possess her; completely, not in a "boy-conquers-girl kind of way," but in an "I-ache-for-you-so-much kind of way."

Judy understood Dave's love for her because she loved him with the same intensity. But after Ronnie Wilson had called her a bastard in the seventh grade, she vowed to lead a virtuous life. She had explained all of that to Dave a number of times, and he'd say he understood, but then the next time they were parked in the country, his needs continued to overwhelm him. Probably neither of them understood that Dave was unconsciously looking to sex as a salve for all the pent-up pressures in his life.

For 1958/59 season, the starters for the Richland team were Dave as center (a forgone conclusion), Eugene as a guard, and a kid named Norman as the other guard. Another guy named Max was a forward, and the second forward was a big surprise to the whole town: Ronnie Wilson.

Coach Robey had taken a good look at his team pre-season and knew they were at a height disadvantage. After Dave's 6'1", the next tallest was Max at 5'10". Ronnie Wilson, who up to this point had not played ball, had inherited his father's height, plus an inch. That put him at 6'3".

The coach decided it would be worth working with a kid as difficult as Ronnie. He didn't have any illusions that Ronnie would ever learn to shoot, but with his height advantage, if he could get himself near the basket, the ball would come to him as often as not. Then he could pass it to someone who could shoot.

When the coach approached Ronnie about playing, Ronnie's response was a question. "Why has it taken you three years to ask me?"

The coach snapped back, "Look Ronnie, most kids don't need to be asked. They want to be on the team and are willing to work hard to get there. No one's begging you. If you develop a positive attitude and want to play, let me know. Practice starts next week, so it will have to be before then."

Ronnie didn't like the coach having the upperhand. But he did like the idea of the fans and cheerleaders cheering for him. He liked that a lot. So, the day before practice began, he told the coach he wanted to play.

As the season progressed, the coach's assumptions regarding Ronnie proved true. One, the ball often did come to him. Two, he never learned to shoot. Where the coach worked the hardest with Ronnie was in passing the ball, and instructing him to do it quickly before the opposing team had a chance to foul. Fans had reservations about seeing Ronnie Wilson on the floor, but gradually came to accept the coach's decision.

Richland's last game was held at home, with the outcome determining if they'd continue on to the Sectional. That accomplishment was last achieved in 1934, the year Dave's father had been the star of the team. Richland only had bleachers on one side of their gym and they were just eight rows high. Trudy Travis, wearing a red sweater two sizes too small, sat in the second row to cheer Ronnie on.

 Anticipating correctly that practically everyone in town and the surrounding countryside would be in attendance, additional bleachers were erected on the stage.

Cardinal fans, attending regular games, maintained a constant state of excitement, but tonight's game was head-exploding. Judy and the other cheerleaders, wearing cardinal red uniforms, stood in front of the fans and chanted, "Red and White, fight, fight, fight! Red and White, fight, fight, fight."

But with only seventy-five seconds left in the game, and down six points, it looked daunting. However, they had the ball, and after Max and Norman passed it back and forth, Norman faked an attempt to take it in, only to bring it back out. At this point, so sure Dave would be in the right corner, he threw the ball without even looking. Dave quickly got off a jump shot that rolled around the rim and then went in. Richland was now down by four.

Boswell, the opposing team, called a time out. Once the game resumed, a Boswell guard took the ball downcourt, while their center and forwards put in motion the play the coach had instructed. In addition, the guards were directed to play out the clock and try to draw a foul. But instead, Norman succeeded in stealing the ball, passed it off to Eugene, who drove it to the other end and made a layup. As icing on the cake, he drew a foul in the act of shooting. Richland fans knew he would make it. Richland was now down by a single point.

The tension in the gym was unbelievable. With twenty-seven seconds left on the clock, Boswell once again took the ball downcourt. And once again, they tried running out the clock while attempting to draw a foul. With only six seconds left, the ball was again successfully stolen, this time by Eugene. He instantly threw it to Dave, who bounced it twice on his way to mid-court. He then got the ball off with precision; it was still floating in air when the buzzer sounded.

The ball swished through the basket. The instant pandemonium in the gym had not been seen nor heard in twenty-five years. The fans ran out onto the floor, and two guys unsuccessfully tried lifting Dave up on their shoulders, but he was too tall.

Two other guys were much more successful with Eugene. Judy ran out to give Dave a hug, but she had to wait behind Dave's father who had his arms tightly wrapped around his son. There were tears streaming down Bill's face, and he didn't care who saw them!

The Sectional game was played at Benton, whose gym had the county's largest seating capacity. Richland won their first Sectional game against Ambia, and Benton won their first game against Otterbein. This set up a showdown between Richland and Benton, of which the winner would proceed to the Regionals in Lafayette. Richland had never won a Sectional, and the idea that they could advance to the Regional had every head in town spinning! The concern that Benton had home court advantage was erased by Richland's furious momentum.

The final Sectional game was a nail-biter and by the time it got down to the last sixty seconds, Richland fans were holding their collective breaths. Their team was up by a point, but anything could happen in basketball.

Benton had the ball, and after getting the ball downcourt, a player took a shot from the left side. It hit the board, and bouncing off the board, came right at Ronnie but passed through his fingers. A Benton forward recovered the ball and threw it out to their center positioned beyond the key. He lobbed the ball to the basket, making it. Benton was now up by one point.

Richland called a time-out. Coach Robey instructed his boys, "Norman, bring the ball down. Benton is going to be all over Dave on the left so find Max on the right and get the ball to him. Max, if you have a good shot, take it. If not, throw the ball to Ronnie who will be out by the foul line. That will throw them off; they won't expect that, and it may take one of their guys off Dave. Dave, come in towards Ronnie, then Ronnie, throw the ball to Dave. Dave, I know this won't be one of your tried-and-true shots, but it will confuse Benton's defense all to hell to see you moving in that direction."

Dave declared confidently, "I can make it."

With eighteen seconds left on the clock, Norman brought the ball down and threw it to Max. Max tried going in but had to come back out and to the right. He then threw it to Ronnie who almost lost the ball but held onto it at the last second. Dave broke free and then came running in. With five seconds left he was wide open to receive Ronnie's pass.

But instead of passing the ball, and with the clock ticking away, Ronnie decided to take the last shot himself. His effort was tragic; the ball went over the bank board.

Benton fans screamed in exhilaration and a good many burst out laughing; they just couldn't help it. Richland fans were stunned into silence. Again, Dave's father had tears streaming down his cheeks and again, he didn't care who saw them.

....

With basketball season behind them, and the dream of finally winning a sectional tournament crushed, thoughts turned to the three school rituals of spring: the prom, the school play, and graduation. It was automatically assumed that Judy and Dave would go to the prom together.

One afternoon, as Dave and Eugene were walking out of school, Dave said, "I suppose you'll be taking Wanda to the prom."

With a doubtful look on his face, Eugene replied, "I haven't asked her yet...I don't know that I am."

Dave asked, "Why? What's going on?"

"I'm going to surprise you by using a word you probably don't think I know. Wanda is just too vacuous."

"You're using a word I don't know. What does vacuous mean?"

"Empty. Empty-headed, as in nothing going on up there. Her idea of an interesting conversation is about Elizabeth Taylor, Eddie Fisher, and Debbie Reynolds. Only she refers to them on a first name basis. Their messy lives hold no end of fascination for her."

"But surely you're going to go to the prom. It's our senior year."

"Dave, you know what I'm thinking? I'm thinking of asking Linda. She's so bright; and I'm sure we'd find a lot to talk about."

"Wow! I love that idea. The two of you could double with Judy and me. I know Judy would be thrilled. We'll have a really great time!"

The privilege of decorating for the prom was limited to juniors and seniors. A prom committee had already made basic decisions such as that year's theme, "Stairway to Heaven," and the decorating colors, yellow and white. Crepe paper, the main decorating medium, had multiple uses. Strands, strung in a curling fashion from the sides to the middle, could form a canopy. The paper could also be hung as streamers, hiding anything that might diminish the evening's mood. And it could be used to make flowers, huge bouquets of flowers, lavishly interspersed throughout the room. An important tradition was, once the decorating was under way, the doors had to be closed at all times to keep the magic under wraps.

When Dave arrived to pick Judy up the night of the prom, she did indeed look magical. She was wearing a daisy yellow, floor length, princess dress that perfectly blended with her blonde hair. Dave had always thought her beautiful, but tonight she was breathtaking. The corsage he had brought, dominated by white carnations, was the perfect compliment.

Upon arriving at the prom, Judy's magic continued to exude. The colors of her dress and corsage made it look as if the whole affair had been decorated for her. The subdued lighting formed by spotlights of soft yellow and white only added to her spell.

What made this a special prom was that they were able to secure "4 Hits and a Miss," a band that usually played more sophisticated venues. A nice surprise toward the end of the evening, and tying in with the prom's theme, the band performed Neal Sedaka's current hit, "Stairway to Heaven."

The band leader, Bun Walkup, crooned,

"I'll build a stairway to heaven,

I'll climb to the highest star,

I'll build a stairway to heaven

Cause heaven is where you are..."

Chapter Eleven: Aspirations

After Dave dropped Eugene and Linda off, he and Judy drove to their favorite parking place in the country. Judy had clearly been the knockout of the evening, and maybe that's why Dave's desires were at an all-time peak. But it may have also been Dave's fear that the future was not looking kindly on their love, and this trepidation drove his overwhelming need to finally possess her entirely.

As he became more and more aggressive, he uttered in a voice tinged with desperation, "Judy, I love you more than you can ever know. Doesn't that mean anything?"

Judy, who was also caught up into the escalating passion replied softly, "I love you, too," and then Dave pushed her down on the seat and positioned himself on top of her. Suddenly, Judy felt her body go from hot to cold. She cried out, "Get off of me!" Dave ignored her request. She repeatedly pleaded with him as she tried pushing him off. But the harder she pushed, the more he resisted. Finally she reached up and slapped him across the face.

That got his attention. As he sat up, he said, "That wasn't necessary."

When Judy was able to right herself, she replied, "I'm afraid it was."

"You could have simply told me to stop."

"What are you talking about? I pleaded with you! All of a sudden, I don't feel safe with you."

Dave's reply was a sulking presence.

Judy responded by putting her shoes on and saying, "Pout all you want. I'm going to walk home." With that she got out of the car and slammed the door.

Dave drove off leaving a trail of dust. Twelve minutes later, after he had driven around the square mile of a country section, he came up from behind. He stopped, rolled down the window, and said, "You don't have to talk to me, but get in, and I'll drive you home. For what's it worth, I'm sorry." Judy did get in, but it was a silent ride until he reached her home, whereupon she hastily let herself out of the car.

They couldn't avoid seeing each other in school as they were in the same classes, but Judy wasn't in any mood to talk with

Dave. Then two weeks after the prom, Dave called Judy on a Saturday morning, and at least she didn't hang up. He said, "Judy, when I said I was sorry, I really meant it. I hope you know that by now." Dave took a couple of breaths and continued, "But I'm not calling to ask you out; I don't think I deserve that yet. I'm calling you because you're my best friend, and I was hoping you'd be willing to take a walk with me this afternoon. If it's okay with you, I want to drive out and walk along Anstett Road. We could start out where Sugar Creek passes through it."

Judy, whose heart had been warming toward Dave, hadn't known how to break their impasse. She was relieved with the offer and replied, "What time are you thinking about?"

"Would 4:00 be too late?"

"No, that will be fine."

With an unusual flare of emotion in his voice, he exclaimed, "Oh, Judy, I'm just so happy to hear your voice! I'll see you at 4:00."

 When Dave arrived, Judy could sense there was something serious on his mind. Whatever it was, apparently she would have to wait, because for the time being, he was attempting to exchange pleasantries. He asked about what she had been doing that day, how her mother was, how Mrs. Thorton was, etc.

When they finally reached the point where Dave parked the car, they got out and started walking. Dave continued being silent for a good five minutes, and Judy began to wonder if he could find it in him to talk about what was on his mind.

Finally, he said, "Just take a deep breath. Don't you find the fragrances of spring in the countryside almost overwhelming?"

Judy smiled but remained silent, suspecting he had more to say.

Dave pointed to a guy out in the nearby field, and said, "That's Pinky Anstett pulling a cultivator. I can just feel his euphoria. He's spent the winter fixing his equipment to get back in the fields and there he is, feeling this warm spring breeze, and inhaling the rich smells of the overturned soil. He knows another crop is on its way, and that he'll participate in every part of it.

"You know what's funny? Eugene can't wait to get off the farm. His older brother will take it over anyway, but Eugene can't wait to go to college and then probably law school after that.

"But Judy, I've always loved coming out into the country and walking along these roads. The land is as flat as can be, and I know a city person would say to me, "Man, what are you looking at?" Dave reflected a few seconds and then resumed, "But if they can't see it, there wouldn't be any use in me telling them. What I'm looking at is the huge unobstructed sky right down to the ground, with ever-changing cloud formations floating by, sunsets painted with every color known to man, plus those he doesn't know because he can't keep up with the miracle of it, and a sense that as one day fades, another one will arrive tomorrow, just as unique in its own way.

"And then some days, I spend more time studying all the plant life growing by the roadside." He stopped for a few seconds to point out some of his favorites. "See these lacy flowers; they're asters. And this group of purple-looking daisies are called brandywine. The yellow-looking daisies are called cup plants. Then, of course, there's plenty of purple and white clovers. And, look at the little white moth feeding off the clover; it's God's beautiful garden set on the side of a gravel road."

Judy finally interjected, "Dave, a few weeks ago, under less pleasant circumstances, I told you that I didn't know who you were. I'll say the same again today. Only now I'm hearing a poet who can look at an empty field and make it come to life with smells and textures, someone who can look at the sky and see continuous mystery. And Dave, you've learned to look at the hidden beauty of the roadside with an artist's eye. I feel so honored that you're sharing this with me."

"I just had to share it with you! I'm just bursting with it. Being out in the country; this is who I am. This sense, this identity, has been building up in me for years, but I never felt I could share it with anyone. My family, my dad in particular, has pegged me as a doctor as long as I can remember. It's not what I want to do. But maybe his idea of me enlisting into the army for four years so that I can get the GI Bill benefits isn't such a bad one. That would give me four years to figure out what I really could do with my life."

Judy mused, "I'm going through a similar situation. Mom's envisioned me in a nursing uniform since I could walk. I'm not saying I don't want to be a nurse, but I don't know if I want to, either. On top of that, Mom's lived her whole life for me; I don't know if I could disappoint her.

They both fell into an easy silence, the kind of quiet when you hear the birds chirping and, on this day, the sound of Pinky Anstett's tractor moving through the field. They walked for another fifteen minutes, both lost in their thoughts.

Then Dave said, "I don't think we're going to figure out the rest of our lives today. What would you say if we ran over to Newton and grabbed a custard cone at Schultz's Root Beer Stand? We're already headed in that direction."

With an inviting smile, Judy replied, "I'd love it."

The following Monday, as Judy arrived at the Jewell House, she took notice of the music room to the right of the entrance foyer. It often caught her attention as it was dominated by a grand piano which Irene had bought to impress her guests. But outside of Lillian's daughter Marie, who had pounded on the keys now and then, the only one who had really played it was Arthur.

Judy had always looked at the instrument enviously, and one day got up the nerve to ask Lillian if she could play it. Lillian hadn't known that Judy played, and that only added to a list of qualities for which she admired the girl. Lillian replied, "Of course you can play it. But do you realize that no one has seriously played that instrument in almost sixty years? First, let me have it tuned for you."

Judy replied, "Mrs. Thorton, I didn't mean for you to go through so much trouble."

Lillian responded, "I want to do it, and I'm going to get someone from Chicago who would know what to do with an instrument that old. It would mean a lot to me to hear that instrument come to life again."

Once the piano was tuned, Judy would arrive a half hour early so that she could play. She never dreamed that music directed by her fingers on the keyboard could reach such perfection. Usually, she played popular tunes she had already learned. She had chosen carefully to play songs such as "Come Softly to Me," "The Twelfth of Never," "Lonesome Town," music she judged would not be too jarring if Mrs. Thorton was listening from upstairs.

One day Lillian was in a meeting with her attorney Nathan Bark, and out of the blue, Lillian heard the song "The Faded Flower." She mused to Nathan, "How could that girl know that song? That was a favorite of Arthur's."

Then Lillian said something of a more personal nature than Nathan Bark had ever heard her express. "Oh, I wish she was my granddaughter! She has brought such joy into this house."

Later that evening, Lillian asked Judy how she had learned to play such an old song. Judy replied that it was something Mrs. Cook had taught her early in her lessons, and that she had loved playing it ever since.

Judy continued to read stock quotes and futures' values to Lillian, but now Lillian would go into detailed explanations as to why that data was meaningful to her. Judy also poured over the broadcast trade journals, keenly absorbed by which stations were generating the most advertising revenue. No one else had ever seemed so interested, not even her long-time-secretary, Dorothy.

Judy also had become very curious as to how Lillian chose the beneficiaries of her charitable giving. It forced Lillian to think back to the beginning and see a pattern. From her days when she attended Evanston College for Women, she had been aware of the suffering of the urban poor, and particularly the plight of women and children. She had theorized that men had a better chance of surviving on their own, as many did after abandoning their families.

One day, while Trudy was working her shift, Nathan Bark came for an appointment. Trudy could not have been more surprised when he asked her to serve as a witness for a new will to be drawn for Mrs. Thorton. The other witness was Mr. Bark.

In essence, the will left $10,000 outright to Dorothy Ziegler, $5,000 outright to Judy Bennett, plus an education fund for Judy Bennett to pursue any education of her choosing. Of the remaining value of the estate, thirty percent of Lillian's holding were to be invested into a fund that would distribute earnings to Lillian's charities in future years. The residual seventy percent would go to her grandson, Ronald Wilson.

Trudy could not wait for her shift to end so that she could tell Ronnie the good news. Both were elated. They knew of Lillian's antipathy for her grandson, but apparently, the old adage, "Blood is thicker than water," held true. They took delight in anticipation that those in the community who Ronnie didn't like, which was everyone, would have to live with the reality that the line of wealth, begun by his great, great, great grandfather, Edward Henry, had been passed on to him.

However, Ronnie's elation was qualified. He reacted, "Who does the old lady think she is! I'll fight that will to get my hands on the other thirty percent of my money. And Dorothy and Judy can forget it!"

Now that they were assured that Ronnie was the major heir, it took Ronnie and Trudy just a few weeks to grow impatient.

How much longer could his grandmother hold on?

This eagerness prompted Trudy to come up with a plan. She had been eavesdropping long enough as Lillian's caretaker to hear Dr. Cotton say repeatedly, "Mrs. Thorton, more than anything, you have to avoid any situation that would give you a sudden shock."

Trudy's idea was to provoke such a shock. She had never liked Judy Bennett. In principle, she didn't like the goody-goody cheerleader type, but she was also jealous that Mrs. Thorton had included Judy in her will. So Trudy's plan was for Ronnie to be waiting for Judy in the entrance foyer that afternoon, and once Judy walked through the door, he was to sic Ajax on her. The girl couldn't help but scream.

Chapter Twelve: Ajax Leaps into Action

Ajax's leap did provoke Judy to scream. But within seconds, Judy punched Ajax in the snout, and the supposedly ferocious dog whimpered away. Ronnie stood there stunned. He expected Ajax to chew Judy to mush, but his teeth marks didn't even break her skin.

However, their dastardly plan had worked.

Trudy came running down the steps. She exclaimed in the best panic-stricken voice she could muster, "I'm afraid the screaming was too much for poor Mrs. Thorton. It appears she has passed on. We need to get Dr. Cotton over here immediately."

Judy was grief stricken, but that didn't prevent her from quick action. She hurried toward the back of the house to use the kitchen phone.

Once Judy was out of earshot, Trudy exclaimed, "Ding Dong, the Witch is Dead. Which old Witch, the Wicked Witch! Ding Dong the Wicked Witch is Dead!" She and Ronnie burst out laughing.

Dr. Cotton arrived within a few minutes, and confirmed that Lillian had indeed passed on. After he left, Ronnie called Nathan Bark.

He said, "The old lady kicked, and I want my money RIGHT NOW. Not tomorrow, but RIGHT NOW."

Mr. Bark replied, "Mr. Wilson, thank you for notifying me of your grandmother's death; she was a great lady and I'm sorry for your loss."

Ronnie's voice became excitable as he shouted, "You're not listening to me! I want my money today!"

"I'm afraid that isn't possible, Mr. Wilson. Your grandmother left instructions that her will was not to be read until after her funeral service."

"Who cares what the old bitch wanted. She's dead!"

"Mr. Wilson, I'm the executor of the will, and I'm afraid I'm going to have to abide by her wishes."

"Well, get this. I just fired you as her executor and naming myself! What do you say to that?"

"Mr. Wilson, there is a legal avenue to pursue such a path, but it will take a matter of weeks at the minimum."

Ronnie exclaimed in exasperation, "So, okay. Let's have the funeral this evening and get it over with."

"Mr. Wilson, your grandmother left precise instructions about how she wanted her service performed, and as her executor, I intend to carry those out."

Before Ronnie slammed the phone down, he screamed, "Just remember. YOU'RE TOAST!"

As would have been expected, Lillian's funeral was by invitation only. It was a small gathering; she had kept in touch with few relatives and even fewer friends.

First on her list of instructions was that the service be conducted in the entrance foyer of the house, and that her casket be placed exactly where Arthur's had rested in 1902. There was also a request that Judy play "The Faded Flame," the song that Arthur had so loved. Mr. Bark gave a brief eulogy. Ronnie was in attendance. However, his attitude suggested that he was there more to stare down Nathan Bark, than to show respect for his grandmother.

The minister from the Presbyterian church conducted a graveside service, and as soon as Lillian's casket was laid to rest, Ronnie approached Mr. Bark, and demanded that the will be read within the hour. Mr. Bark replied, "It will be read tomorrow at my office. Other beneficiaries need sufficient time to arrange their schedules." As Mr. Bark turned to leave, Ronnie could not see the self-satisfying smile on the lawyer's face. Mr. Bark thought to himself, "Young Mr. Wilson is in for the surprise of his life tomorrow!"

A dramatic change of course had commenced ten weeks earlier...all due to machinations initiated by Mr. Bark. He had heard Lillian say, "Oh. I wish Judy was my grandchild," and it got him thinking. Mr. Bark had been around the Thorton family long enough to remember Richard, and the more he looked at Judy, the more he saw Richard. It wasn't just her blonde hair and blue eyes; it was a certain way they both looked at people."

Mr. Bark had also known of Richard's attachment to Helen Bennett. He likewise knew the date Richard had left for the

Pacific War, based on a telegram sent from San Francisco. But what if Richard didn't leave on that date? What if he really left several months later?

Nathan, at his own expense, hired an investigator to pour through old War Department records, hoping to find that the date of Richard's deployment had deliberately been misrepresented. He so hoped he could deliver Mrs. Thorton a wonderful surprise.

The report that came back from the investigator stated that Richard had actually departed the country almost three months later than what had been understood. And Mr. Bark was pretty sure why Richard had used the deception of a misleading telegram.

At a time when Mr. Bark knew Judy would be with Mrs. Thorton, he phoned Helen. She immediately knew who he was; everyone knew of the Barks of *Bark and Bark*. He said, "Helen, I hope you don't mind my calling you by your first name, but I feel like I know you because I've gotten to know Judy so well. I'd like to drop by to see you, but it would be best if Judy wouldn't be home."

Helen was surprised, but not alarmed. Judy had spoken highly of Nathan Bark on several occasions. She replied, "How about tomorrow night about this same time. Would that work?"

"Yes. Thank you for making yourself available."

The following evening Mr. Bark and Helen met. She was surprised at his appearance, that for his height, he was such a spare man. After initial greetings, Mr. Bark said, "Helen, I'll get right to the point. I've done some research through the War Department and discovered that Richard Thorton had additional training at Camp Lejeune and actually deployed for the Pacific on July 5, 1942. I also know that Judy was born on January 18, 1943, approximately six months later. And to be more direct, I strongly suspect that Richard was her father."

Helen's usual calm demeanor deserted her. How does one respond to the breach of an eighteen-year-old secret?

Mr. Bark offered an understanding smile and continued, "Please allow me to explain why I'm injecting myself into a matter that is clearly none of my business. It is because I have heard Lillian

Thorton state more than once how much she wishes that Judy was her granddaughter. She doesn't suspect that to be possible; it's just an intense wish she has. Imagine what joy it would bring her to find out that Judy is her granddaughter. But I would never presume to tell her unless you gave me permission. And if you do allow me, I'd also like to arrange a meeting between the two of you.

Helen finally spoke. She asked, "Could you call me again tomorrow night, after I've had a day to think about it?" Her question tacitly confirmed Mr. Bark's suspicions.

When he did call the following evening, Helen agreed to meet with Lillian. She also agreed that it would be best if Mr. Bark told Lillian beforehand that Judy was, indeed, her grandchild. Mr. Bark then suggested that Helen explain to Mrs. Thorton the particulars of Richard's last months in the United States.

Thornton Wilder's perennial play, "Our Town," was being presented Friday evening at the school, and both Judy and Ronnie would be in attendance. This would allow time for Lillian and Helen to meet. That it was this play held a certain irony. An assignment given Richard during his senior year, he had felt it spoke directly to him, telling him he didn't need to explore the greater world when he had already found his true love at home.

Helen had never been inside the Jewell House; very few townspeople ever had. As she passed through the gate, she momentarily looked to the drive located east of the house, and for a flash, saw

Richard's 1938 yellow Ford coupe. It sent a pang of heartache through her.

She climbed the porch stairs, approached the double doors, and knocked. Much to her surprise, Lillian answered it. She knew who Lillian was, as everyone in town had spotted her one time or another, most usually passing by in a car. But she had hardly expected her to be on the first level; Judy had always described her being in her bedroom suite. She didn't understand at that moment that Lillian had dismissed everyone in the house so that their meeting would be totally private.

The two women just looked at each other for a brief moment before Lillian said invitingly, "Let's go into the music room." Once they were both seated, Lillian said, "My, dear, I hardly know where to begin."

Helen replied with a quiet smile and then Lillian continued. "I'm so grateful that you agreed to come. I could very well understand why you might not."

Helen spoke, "Judy has spoken so highly of you, and I appreciate how good you have been to her."

At the mention of Judy's name, Lillian began to cry, the first time she had shed tears in years. Between her sobs, she said, "I don't think you can imagine how happy I am to learn that Richard was Judy's father. Knowing that makes me feel my life has not been in vain."

Then, collecting herself, she professed, "Oh, I can hardly imagine how presumptuous it must be for you to hear me say such a thing. You of all people, who has done such a wonderful job raising her!"

Lillian had a reflective look as she resumed, "Judy is who I would have liked to have been if I could have waved a wand and made it so. I, who had every luxury, grew up with a very hard heart, a guarded heart at best, and I have remained that way all my life. But to see Judy who is so loving..." Lillian's whimpers again stopped her flow of words.

Helen responded soothingly, "You're not being fair to yourself. You loved Richard, and I certainly know he loved you. I suspect there was a lot of you in him, and I know there's a lot of Richard in Judy."

Lillian, always an organized individual, had pre-planned what topics she wanted to discuss. But before proceeding, she took a deep sigh and then said, "Helen, let me go back twenty years. I owe you such an apology for reproaching Richard for seeing you. He told me I was a snob and he was right. I had a mother who lived and breathed the significance of social distinctions, and my brother Arthur and I suffered greatly because of it. To think I turned around to do the same thing. I should have trusted Richard's judgment and allowed him to bring you home so that Thomas and I could have met you." Lillian smiled at Helen as she continued, "Judy hadn't been in this house thirty minutes before I realized how wrong I was about you."

After another pause, she resumed, "I've never been very good at apologizing. I'm sorry to say that when you have a lot of money, you really don't feel you have to.

But, it would mean so much to me to apologize to you. Can you ever forgive me?"

Helen, who had been listening attentively, replied, "Of course I can. And thinking back, I don't know if I was ever angry with you. Those social distinctions you mentioned, you have to realize that people from below, looking up, understand about such things. My father was a good man, but he was one of your tenant farmers, and he drank too much. I understood those considerations would color your impression of me. But I also thought that would change in time."

Lillian responded, "And finally, so they have!"

Lillian had a hesitant look on her face before moving onto the next topic. She said, "You don't owe the slightest explanation about anything, but Nathan told me that you might fill in the details between the time I thought Richard had deployed and when he actually did."

Helen knew this question would be coming and was ready. She began by saying, "Richard found out about FLEX, which stood for special fleet landing exercises; a program that trained for reconnaissance patrols and landing raids. He knew immediately he had to be part of it because he felt so strongly that the United States had to turn the tables on Japan after their sneak attack on Pearl Harbor. He wanted to be on the forefront of that mission.

"The special FLEX training would keep him at Camp Lejeune for another three months, and he came up with a plan by which he and I could spend a couple of weekends together. He had a buddy from basic training who he knew was about to ship out to the Pacific. He asked him to send that telegram to you. Richard wanted you to think he had shipped out because he didn't want you to be hurt knowing he preferred spending time with me. We met in Lexington, Kentucky for our two weekends. I was able to work my schedule around at the Post House so that no one would miss me.

"Six weeks after he really did deploy, I discovered I was pregnant. I didn't know how I was going to handle the situation other than I was sure I'd have the baby and keep it.

"Then came that horrible day! I was working at the Post House when an older woman from Richland came in to catch a bus. I knew who she was, but I don't think she knew me. Anyway, she said to someone ...and I can hear every word as if she said it yesterday...'Did you hear that Richard Thorton was killed? Somewhere in the Pacific is all they know. I guess all that money isn't going to do him much good now.'

"I froze. I thought about telling my boss that I wasn't feeling well and ask to go home. Then I decided that being by myself would be worse, so I stayed at work. I was a little over three months along at the time, and almost immediately, I realized how grateful I was to have a baby on the way that would always connect me to Richard."

Lillian's last topic on her agenda also took courage, but she continued, "Helen, I know I never gave you any reason to think I might have been helpful, but did you ever consider reaching out to me?"

Helen replied, "No, Mrs. Thorton, I never did. At first I thought the issue would turn on the fact that I couldn't prove that Richard was Judy's father, and I knew I didn't want to be caught up in that kind of dispute.

"But now I'm going to be blunt. In time, I became convinced that I could do a better job raising her completely on my own. It's not that I didn't realize that Richard loved you, and that you loved Richard, but I never thought of the Jewell house as a happy house. There was always something about it, something too detached to think of it as a home."

Lillian listened to this explanation with equanimity and responded, "You were very perceptive, my dear. This monument, built to appease my parents' vanity, has never been a home, and sadly, I think the scars of my childhood always prevented me from making it one.

"And Helen, there's another point that you are kind enough not to mention; I would have wanted a strong hand in making decisions affecting the direction of Judy's life. You've done such a fabulous job on your own; no doubt I would have interfered."

The two women knew their visit had to be limited; Ronnie would soon be returning home. As they said their goodbyes, Lillian reached out to hug Helen, a totally uncharacteristic gesture on her part. Then, as Helen was walking toward the door, she noticed that Lillian appeared unsteady. She asked, "Would you like help getting up the stairs?"

"Yes, dear, I would."

Helen assisted her, and once they reached the second floor, Lillian gave Helen a second unexpected hug. With that, Helen descended the steps.

As she was going out the door, she reflected, "Lillian was so different than the persona of local legend, but knowing her through Judy the past sixteen months prepared me for that. However, the Lillian of the past half hour was so much more vulnerable than I could ever have imagined." Helen wished that she had initiated the second hug, as she surmised that Lillian had very few in her life.

That evening Lillian called Nathan Bark. He was scheduled to come the following afternoon to assist in the making of a new will. Lillian had been thinking for several weeks of making Judy her major beneficiary, and learning that Judy was her granddaughter solidified that intention. However, she had a nagging concern.

She said to Mr. Bark, "As we've discussed, I plan to designate Judy as my major beneficiary, but Trudy's a snoop. If she somehow finds out about the new will, I honestly think it could put Judy's life in danger. Trudy is not to be trusted."

She paused for a second before continuing, "When I first took responsibility for Ronnie, I was looking for an adult companion who would shape his character. In retrospect, I'm afraid I have. Trudy is evil and so is Ronnie."

Mr. Bark, suspecting that Lillian had already thought up a solution to protect Judy, asked, "How do you suggest we handle this?"

"What I think we should do is make two wills tomorrow. The first will leave the bulk of my estate to Ronnie. To make sure Trudy is informed, ask her to be the second witness. You know she'll go straight to Ronnie with the news.

"Then after she leaves, we'll make the final will. We'll ask Dr. Cotton to be present and act as the second witness. Having a lawyer as one witness and a doctor as the second will make it very difficult to challenge. Both its legal legitimacy and my soundness of mind should stand up in court."

Nathan saw the wisdom of such a plan. He had been around Trudy enough to know she was capable of anything. And on a personal basis, he had a strong dislike for Ronnie. He reflected with satisfaction, "Boy, oh boy, what fun it will be when Ronnie finds out he'll have to go out into the world and make a living!"

It was only twenty-three days later when Judy's scream provoked Lillian's fatal heart attack. She was seventy-three years old.

The day following Lillian's funeral, Ronnie and Judy arrived at the Law Offices of *Bark and Bark* simultaneously. Judy said, "Ronnie, don't think I don't know you sicced Ajax on me so that I'd scream and provoke your grandmother's heart attack. You are..."

Ronnie sarcastically interrupted by singing, "La la la la la la la la la la la la la la la la..."

Judy, in turn, cut him off, saying, "You are really sick, Ronnie. I should feel sorry for you, but right now, that's asking a bit much."

He retorted, "Judy, I wouldn't bother coming in if I were you. Whatever my grandmother left you, I'm going to have it revoked."

Gathered in *Bark and Bark's* conference room were Ronnie, Judy, Dorothy Ziegler, and a younger lawyer from the firm. Mr. Bark proceeded to read the will:

"I, Lillian Ruth Thorton, a legal adult with an address at 360 Henry Street, Richland, Indiana, being of competent and sound mind, do hereby declare this to be my last will and testament on this date, May 5, 1959, 7:00 P.M., and do hereby revoke any and all wills and codicils heretofore made jointly or made separately by me.

"To my faithful secretary, Dorothy Ziegler, I leave $10,000 outright. I leave $5,000 outright to my grandson, Ronald Wilson, plus a college education fund to be administered by *Bark and Bark* if Ronald chooses to use it."

At this juncture, Ronnie shot up, shouting, "No way. I know what her will says, and that's not it. I don't know what you're trying to pull, but it won't work."

Mr. Bark responded, "Mr. Wilson, the will you're referring to was superseded by this one. This will was made at a later time."

Ronnie then walked around to where Mr. Bark was seated and tried to grab the will out of his hand. The second lawyer in attendance pulled him away.

Mr. Bark said, "Mr. Wilson, if you can't control yourself, we will call the police and have you removed." Ronnie continued his menacing stance. In a stronger voice, Mr. Bark asserted, "By controlling yourself, I mean you are to be seated as the other beneficiaries are seated." Ronnie finally sat down, and Mr. Bark continued reading the will.

"Of the remaining value of my estate, thirty percent is to be invested into a fund, the earnings of which will continue to support charities listed in a separate codicil attached to this will. The remaining seventy percent is bequeathed to Judy Bennett who has brought great joy into my life."

Ronnie jumped up again and started screaming and cursing. Mr. Bark exclaimed in a raised voice. "This kind of behavior is not to be tolerated," and instructed his associate to call the police. By the time they arrived, Ronnie had left.

Epilogue

After the will was read and Ronnie had fled the conference room, a bewildered Judy asked, "Why did Mrs. Thorton leave all this money to me?"

Mr. Bark replied, "She was very, very, fond of you, Judy. But there's more to the story. To understand that, I think it's best to go home and talk with your mother."

It would be quite a day for Judy: first, to find out that she was now a very, very wealthy young woman, and then discover from her mother that Richard Thorton, who became a war hero, had been her father. Most importantly, she learned that her conception was the fruit of deep love.

News of Mrs. Thorton's will, leaving Judy Bennett as the major beneficiary, spread like wildfire, as did the news that Richard Thorton had been Judy's father. For people whose main focus was gossip, neither revelation was particularly satisfying. They much preferred stories with tainted endings. It was also most unsatisfying not to learn the amount of Judy's inheritance. However, if they guessed the amount to be slightly below seven million dollars after taxes, they would have been close.

Trudy was out of a job, and Ronnie had no intention of sharing one penny of his inherited $5,000. But in a dismal kind of way, Trudy had always been a survivor, and soon ran off with a stranger she met at Tom's Tap. Trudy was soon forgotten in Richland. She hadn't been from there and had never really been "of there," in the way people whose families had lived there for generations were.

Ronnie used $3,300 of his money to buy a red Ford Thunderbird convertible, and then he and Ajax took off to a destination unknown. Eventually he contacted the Richland elevator to forward his modest monthly check, the legacy from his grandfather's will. It was to be sent to a post office box in Bishop, California.

Helen and Vernon became engaged. Strangely, it was only once Judy knew her father's identity that Helen could finally let go of Richard. In his quiet way, Vernon had always understood Helen needed time to work out whatever was holding her back.

The rumors that he had been Judy's father, and that it had all come about as he traveled by bus to Great Lakes for basic training, had eventually reached their ears. It gave them a good laugh.

Both Judy and Dave decided to enroll for fall classes in Purdue's Krannert Business School. Dave would study Agricultural Economics and Judy, General Business, with an emphasis on Finance.

Linda would also enroll at Purdue to pursue a degree in Accounting and was able to do so with a loan from Judy. Eugene would pursue his dream of becoming a lawyer by starting out as an undergraduate at Indiana University in Bloomington.

Judy and Dave knew they had found their life partner. Marriages right out of high school were not uncommon in Richland, and the young couple saw no reason to wait.

The wedding was held in the front yard of the Jewell House. The early September day turned out to be pleasantly moderate, and there were wistful clouds in the sky, which did not go unnoticed by Dave. The invitation was open: everyone in the town, plus the families from local farms.

Judy made her entrance through the front doors onto the porch. Accompanied by a recording of Mendelssohn's "Wedding March" piped through an open window of the music room, she descended the wide front steps.

Her dress created quite a stir; it was the same wedding dress Lillian had worn in 1920. It was a floor length lace gown with a scoop neck and a sweeping train. Judy looked breathtaking!

However, the real thrill for Judy was knowing it had been worn by Lillian! Her grandmother, Lillian!

With a bride as radiant as Judy, it would be easy to overlook the groom. Unless of course he was movie star handsome, as Dave appeared in his white dinner jacket.

Judy, knowing she could afford any extravagance for her wedding, kept it a simple affair. She very much wanted her guests to feel comfortable. There were sandwiches of ham salad and chicken salad, coleslaw and potato salad, and, of course, cake, ice cream, punch, and mints. It was the kind of fare that would be served at other Richland weddings.

She also wanted to satisfy everyone's curiosity. To that end, guests were free to roam through the entire house from basement to the famed third floor ballroom that had been talked about for generations. All and all, it was a grand day for Richland that would be talked about for years to come.

Judy, Dave, and Linda commuted daily to Purdue by car, and their college years flew quickly. A year after her graduation, Judy had gained enough confidence to expand Lillian's broadcast holdings. She also gave generously to charities she felt most worthy. And because she had been part of the community in ways Lillian never had, Judy also supported efforts closer to home.

Dave ran the farm operations and installed the most modern facilities known to raise livestock. However, when it was time for planting and harvesting, Dave immersed himself into the field work, and was totally one with all the sensual perceptions that meant so much to him.

Eugene eventually joined the firm of *Bark and Bark*, and Judy was his biggest client. Linda worked for a firm in Lafayette and handled Judy and Dave's accounting needs. Sometime in their mid-twenties, Eugene and Linda resumed dating and were married by year's end.

Judy and Dave had a very good marriage. They had five children, two boys and three girls, within eleven years. The kids and their friends were constantly running all through the house from top to bottom.

With the exception of the music room, Judy and Dave made significant alterations throughout the Jewell House. The first transition was to update the master bedroom suite. They replaced Lillian's furniture with furnishings of their liking, but most importantly, it became Dave's room as much as Judy's. They also converted Lillian's attached office space into a cozy sitting room. What had been Cyrus's room and then Thomas's, became a large office space for Judy and Dave with plenty of room for two secretaries.

The oblong living room, which had been the least preferred space in the house, now became the favorite. It was converted into a playroom for the kids, which included a children's library, shelved on the south wall, a ping pong table, a pool table, and plenty of space for running around. The most comfortable furniture was retained and grouped at the west end to form a family room.

The ridiculously large dining room, which had hardly been used in the history of the house, was separated into two rooms. The one just off the playroom became a living room where Judy and Dave could entertain friends, and at the same time, keep an eye on the kids. The second new room, which opened to the kitchen, became an appropriately-sized dining room.

The ballroom had various uses, but an event that could be counted on year after year occurred just before Christmas. Magically decorated for the holiday, the invitees were the tenant families, plus any family in town headed by a single parent. Dave and Judy collected a wish list for the children, encouraging parents to submit extravagant suggestions. Dave never seemed to be there, but if one were to guess Santa's height, he appeared to be around 6'1".

The fence that had surrounded the house for over eighty years was removed, and kids constantly passed though the yard as a shortcut to the park. Behind the house, they often picked berries off the bushes and fruit from the trees. They were very welcome to it.

Lillian would have been pleased. Finally, the Jewell House had become a home.

Acknowledgements:

To my sister Carolyn Benner, who served as editor. To Anji Strasburger, who served as copy editor, to Carolyn Walkup and Christine Walkup, who served as Americana consultants. To my brother Kevin Funk, who served as a basketball consultant. And to Todd Hipsher, who designed the cover and helped with every techy aspect of writing and publishing this book.

Other Books by Edward J. Funk

Biography:

"Behind the Door: the Real Story of Loretta Young"

"Loretta and Me"

"Eavesdropping: Loretta Young Talks about her Movie Years"

"You Reap what they Sowed"

Autobiography:

 "Down a Country Road and Beyond"

Fiction:

"Uncle Wonderful"

"Oh so Charming, Oh so Cruel"

"Christmas Eve on Hwy 41"

 "About a Family..."

www.ingramcontent.com/pod-product-compliance
Lightning Source LLC
Chambersburg PA
CBHW020748250626
47155CB00003B/980